Sweet THING

NEW YORK TIMES BESTSELLING AUTHOR

JA HUSS

ABOUT THE BOOK

SWEET THING is a full-length standalone older-man-very-young-woman sexy romance filled with forbidden lust, too many 'first times' to count, inappropriate touching in public, and an angsty, but perfect, HEA.

**I knew how old she was.
I just didn't care.**

RYKER
Aria Amherst lied about her age the first night we met.
But when I kissed her… I knew exactly how old she was.
And once I kissed her… I needed more.
I wanted all of her. I wanted everything she wasn't really offering.
Until I found out that her father was making a deal with my business partner.

Then I wanted her more.

ARIA
Ryker North blew into my life like a wall of hot, tattooed muscle.
And did I mention he's a drummer?
And a businessman?
And thirty-five years old?

1

And my father is going to kill me when he finds out I'm dating his new client?

It's… complicated.
But take my word on this. He's worth every risk I'm taking.

CHAPTER ONE

"Did you hear me, Aria?" my older sister, April, calls from her bedroom.

"I heard you," I mumble back. I'm looking out her front window, which has a view of the city down below. She's technically on a side street, but this is a corner apartment, so the bustling busyness of State Avenue in the Gingerbread neighborhood is in full view.

I can't believe I get to live here for a month on my own. It's almost too good to be true. I've pinched myself so many times today testing to see if I was dreaming, I have a bruise on my arm.

"What did I say?" April pokes her head out through the open door and taps her foot, irritated.

"You said"—I sigh—"there's some stupid board meeting tonight at the Creative Co-op and I have to attend in your place. I heard you."

She smiles. Right answer.

I cut her some slack. Because she got called away last-minute to go do a series of photoshoots in Australia and now her whole life is up in fantastic disarray because her flight leaves in four hours and she's got twenty minutes left to pack before she has to rush to the airport.

"What else?"

"Feed the cat," I say, reaching over to pet Felix. He meows and arches his back, crying to get more out of the quick rub.

She waggles her finger at me and says, "And no sex parties."

Which makes me huff a laugh. As if I'm even having sex.

"Also, stay away from my toys."

"Gross!"

"You borrow everything else."

"I'm not going to borrow your vibrator, April. You're disgusting."

4

She cackles out a laugh and returns to packing.

We are as different as night and day. She is blonde, and perky, and has an exciting career as an apprentice for a huge fashion photographer. She wears fun clothes, and goes fun places, and has a bazillion fun friends and even funner boyfriends. She is outgoing and bubbly, never afraid to try new things.

Me, on the other hand... I'm what they call the quiet one. I like books and take school seriously. My hair is dark red and no one has ever called me perky and fun. And while I know lots of people and consider most of them acquaintances, I don't really have close friends. No BFF and no one I hang out with after school because I go to school in the city and live an hour away in the suburbs.

Every morning for the past four years I've ridden into the city and back home with my father. And the kids in my neighborhood all go to school locally. So they have their own social circles now. All the kids I used to be friends with back in middle school have moved on and forged new circles of friends. So now, when I'm home, I'm just the girl they used to hang out with.

It's not that no one invites me places, it's just I don't really fit in when I try to hang out. The neighborhood kids are all into their sports. And I have zero interest in going to football and baseball games to cheer on kids I barely know anymore.

And all my city friends have after-school clubs. Or go to the same church, or are members of the same country clubs.

It's just weird and kind of hard to explain. Plus, unlike April, who got a car for her sixteenth birthday and could go places without my father dropping her off and picking her up, I got a spring break trip to Space Camp for my sixteenth birthday. Which was totally fun, but didn't help my social life much.

It's not like I'm complaining. I barely saw my father when I was younger because he worked such long hours and we lived so far from his job. And now we have a great relationship, even if most of our quality time is spent during the morning and evening commute.

Anyway, that's why I don't have a lot of friends to hang out with and why this little adventure in the city is pretty much the highlight of my life.

April and I are different in other ways too. She's one of those artistic people. She draws, and paints, and dances, and plays two instruments. Also very cool. But also… so not me. The total extent of my artistic ability is manipulating photos in Photoshop. But that's just a hobby. I'm thinking about going into banking like my father.

After I finish college, that is.

Well, after I finish high school and then college, that is.

6

But high school barely counts anymore. I have six weeks left and I get to spend almost all of that time here, in April's apartment, taking care of Felix and pretending I'm an adult.

Which almost isn't pretend anymore because my birthday is in two days.

I'm a product of the sprawling, wealthy suburbs, which translates to sheltered, right? I see the real world from the other side of a window while sitting in the passenger seat of my father's Mercedes.

Sure, I am educated in the city but my school is like a little enclave of upper-class safety, so this little house-sitting gig for my sister is mostly a practical exercise as far as my parents are concerned. Next fall I'm going to college in the city near my high school, St. Bernadette of Lourdes Academy, just a few blocks away from here, and they want to make sure I'm prepared for this.

My dad works ten blocks up from the school and April has her office in the Creative Co-op around the corner from her apartment. So this is kinda like our neighborhood. A borrowed one, for sure. But it's all I have and anyway, I love it.

It's cool, and trendy, and there are lots of artists and young people around. The Creative Co-op was founded by my mother and sister so April could afford a photography studio with a swank, up-and-coming address.

7

Hence, the board meeting. I'm her proxy until she comes back and there's a new tenant application to go over tonight. So adulting here I come. *It's trial by fire, Aria.*

I can't wait.

The buzzer rings and April comes rushing out from the bedroom dragging a suitcase with clothes, a trunk with equipment, and her giant shoulder bag.

"I'm coming, I'm coming," she yells at the buzzer.

She stops in front of me, pulls me into a hug, bashing my leg with her carry-on, and kisses my cheek. "Be good and I'll see you in a month!" Then she blows a kiss at Felix, who ignores her, and says, "Bye, bye, kitty!"

I pull the front door open and she rushes through, her friend Kathleen already reaching for her trunk at the top of the stairs.

There are a few more moments of frazzled disarray as they drag the luggage down three flights of stairs and then they rush outside and the world calms down again.

I close the apartment door and lean against it, smiling as I imagine an entire month of *Girls Gone Wild: Aria Edition.*

That makes me snort. But a girl can hope.

My phone buzzes in the front pocket of my skirt and I pull it out to find a text from April.

Don't forget the board meeting!

I text back a thumbs up and slip my phone back into my pocket.

I've been to plenty of board meetings with my father since I started high school. We've always been a pair in the city because he works so close to my school and we commute together. So most days I walk over to his office after school and do homework and sometimes he has to stay late and I'm stuck there listening to him and all his powerful friends discuss investments, and stock, and loans.

So even though I've never been to one of the Creative Co-Op board meetings, I'm pretty sure I can handle it.

Dress smart. Pay attention. Nod my head or shoot disapproving looks as other members debate the issues, then agree or disagree on the vote.

I've got this.

Most of it.

I look down at my clothes and decide the St. Bernadette uniform has to go.

Luckily April and I are the same size. So I go into her bedroom—squealing internally because it's mine for a whole month—and pull open her huge walk-in closet.

9

My father had that made specially for her when he remodeled this apartment and April really knows how to fill up a closet, let me tell you. She's got a whole wall of shoes, and racks and racks of dresses, and skirts, and cool ripped jeans.

Mostly things I would never wear, and almost none of which are appropriate for a board meeting, but anything is better than my uniform. Besides, I've perfected my serious, up-and-coming businesswoman look and I'm positive I can pull together something smart.

It might be a hybrid version of April and Aria, but that's what new opportunities are for, right?

This is the first day of St. Bernadette's spring break and in order to appease my parents' fears about possibly being lonely and isolated while I stayed in the city for a month, I told them I'd take a Photoshop certification class over at the local college while I was on break.

I started retouching April's photographs when she was a freshman in college and it kinda became my thing. Plus, that certification looks good on a college application.

But I have a whole weekend between now and that first class and sadly, this board meeting is the only thing on my agenda aside from my birthday tea with my parents at the Corinthian Hotel on Sunday.

So hello, April's closet. What can you do to help me out here?

CHAPTER TWO

"Ryker!" Ozzy says. "I need one more signature." My best bro and business partner, Oswald Herrington III—otherwise known as Ozzy—thrusts a piece of paper and a pen at me as I try to rush past him to make my meeting.

"I gotta go, man!"

"Just quick," he says, handing me the pen. "Sign. It's just a purchase order for the festival."

The festival is a giant pain in my ass. Ozzy's idea, all of it. But we've finally bought the last piece of property we need to redevelop the Gingerbread neighborhood and people are pissed off about gentrification.

OK, yes, that's exactly what we're doing. But we honestly don't want to kick low-income people out so we can make a boatload of money. We want to lift up the neighborhood for everyone. So this festival is our way of letting the neighborhood know we're all in this together. We want them to stay, enjoy the new safer, trendier neighborhood, and spruce up their aging homes. We're even putting together loan packages so we can help them renovate and raise their property values and become part of the transition.

I don't know if it's working—yet—but we're doing our best to win them over.

When we took on this project we knew some people would be forced out of the neighborhood. But if what we're doing ends up changing all the things that make Gingerbread so interesting, then what's the point? We can restore all the old Victorian houses and paint them up pretty, but people already come to Gingerbread for night life and restaurants and the houses are mostly all shit. People don't come for the houses. They come for the food, and the music, and the art, and the people.

There's a fine line between rehabilitation and annihilation and neither Ozzy nor I want to be on the wrong side of this once it's done.

Which is part of the reason I'm trying to rent a space in the Creative Co-Op. That's where the neighborhood artists *create*.

And I just happen to be a drummer. Well, not since freshman year of college, actually. And that was a good fifteen years ago. But I still have the old kit and I think inserting myself into the artists' community will show the neighborhood I'm one of them.

Ozzy, well, he's not so sure. He's worried about my renewed interest in drumming because of how into the 'scene' I was back when we first met. I had to talk him into spending almost two hundred thousand dollars cash purchasing this creative space and tonight's meeting is Judgment Day. I have to defend my application to the Creative board.

Yeah, it's gonna be a disaster. I can already tell. For one thing, I have to call them Mr. This and Miss That. No first names allowed. Weird and sorta pretentious for a group of artists, if you ask me. But I think they already hate me and that's part of their you're-not-welcome-here plan.

They're totally gonna deny me. And I hate being denied. Fucking hate it. I don't care what that says about my character, it's just a fact. That's why we have all the property in Gingerbread in the first place. I bartered and negotiated until those people decided they couldn't afford to say no.

Not helpful when you're trying to win people over and convince them you're not out to ruin the culture they've carefully cultivated over the past fifty years. But we've got a good plan, we really have.

I sign the paper, thrust the pen back at Ozzy, and rush out the door to my waiting car. It's a good thirty minutes in traffic to get over there and by the time I'm walking into the co-op, I'm stressed, and late, and running my fingers through my hair so the long strands that are usually perfectly groomed kinda hang over in my face.

Just… please. Get me through this ambush with a yes. That's all I'm asking for. One. More. Yes.

"Mr. North, I presume," a man wearing a vintage army jacket and baggy ripped jeans says, as I stop in the lobby and look around.

Hmmm. Interesting place. There's about two dozen offices down the long, wide hallway and each one of them is made of glass on all sides. This gives me a glimpse of my new neighbors as they work. A few are painting. One is doing ballet at a barre. One is playing the violin, swaying back and forth like he's caught in a trance. And one is a goddamn mime—black leotard and scary black and white makeup on her face. Doing that whole glass room thing, even though she's actually *in* a glass room.

What the fuck am I doing? I do not belong here. I'm wearing a ten-thousand-dollar suit, a fifty-thousand-dollar watch, and I was brought to this meeting by my company driver.

"Mr. North?" the man asks again.

"Yes," I say, turning to him. "That's me. But you can call me—"

"Mr. North." The man smiles. "Pleasure to meet you," he says, extending his hand. "I'm Mr. Garcia."

OK. So that's how it's gonna be. "Very nice to meet you, Mr. Garcia. This is a great place. I had no idea it was so… modern."

Mr. Garcia gives me a tight smile that shows zero teeth. "Yes," he says. "The Amherst family put this in about four years ago so Miss Amherst would have a place for her photography studio. And even though they still own the building, we all own our individual offices, which is why we're called the co-op."

"Right," I say, forcing myself to smile—not tightly and with teeth. "That's an amazing concept."

But what I want to say is, *I'm a fucking developer, dude. I know what a co-op is.*

"Everyone else is already here, Mr. North. So if you'd like to follow me into the board room, we can get this meeting underway."

I follow him in and find eight people sitting around a large mahogany table. Garcia pans his hand at the empty chair at the bottom of the table and then walks the length of the room to stand in front of his seat at the top.

"Everyone," he says. "This is Mr. North. The *drummer.*"

And the way he says 'drummer' indicates one of two things. One. He doesn't believe I'm a drummer. I'm just some rich asshole from uptown trying to take over his hood. Or two. I am a drummer and drummers are not welcome here.

Which… I can see his point. Because drums are loud and obnoxious. Not calming and beautiful like the

15

violin. They belong in garages, and bars, and the backs of vans. Not in this apparently highly sophisticated artists' community.

But I'm prepared for that. I've already come up with a solution.

He goes around the table introducing people. Mrs. Chi, Mr. Stratkowski, Miss Lynst, etc. etc. etc. until he ends up at Miss Amherst.

Amherst. As in the people who own the building. As in the spoiled little photographer who needed a trendy place to create.

Normally I'd internally roll my eyes at that, but Miss Amherst is very sexy.

She's wearing a tight, white button-down shirt that gives the impression it's made for a man, but has darts and tucks in all the right places so her ample breasts are stretching the buttons just enough. Not enough so I can get a peek at her bra, but just enough to hint that one tug and all those buttons will come flying off to reveal something truly spectacular.

Her hair is dark red. Not ginger. Not auburn. But burgundy. She's got it up in a tight bun that makes me think she'd look good in that ballerina's leotard and tutu just down the hall.

And she's young. In college, probably.

Which is kinda my thing. Ever since I left my twenties behind—far behind now—I've been drawn to the young ones. Not something I'm particularly proud of, just something I've come to accept about myself.

I nod hello and force myself not to stare at Miss Amherst. Pointedly turning my attention back to Garcia as he begins to talk and ask me questions about why I'd like to buy into the Creative Co-Op.

I answer dutifully. I've prepared a statement and I'm a natural speaker so I don't need notes or anything. Just ramble on about how I lost my creativity during freshman year of college and became interested in business and blah, blah, blah, bullshit, bullshit, bullshit.

All the while I'm secretly gawking at Miss Amherst out of the corner of my eye, wondering what color her bra is.

CHAPTER THREE

"OK," Mr. Garcia says. "Thank you for that, Mr. North."

I like Mr. Garcia so far. He's a painter and he's always drinking beer in his little studio. Even during the day. April talks about him all the time like they are best friends. Actually, everyone here has been really cool about me taking over April's studio for a month to work on my Photoshop skills. They are encouraging and upbeat. Always telling me that I should stay away from my father's banking business and do something fun with my life. Like April is.

It's just... I'm not *that girl*.

I'm just not into fun.

No, that's not true. And it's kinda stupid. Everyone is into fun. It's just that all my acquaintances are like me. Quiet, studious, and Saturday nights are mostly about chatting online or gramming ourselves to make people *think* we're having fun.

I'm not daring, like April. I'm not outgoing or bold.

I'm actually pretty shy. And the way Mr. North is looking at me has my neck all sweaty and my skin all prickly.

The white shirt was a mistake. I knew it was too tight. I'm a size bigger than April in the bra department so my buttons are stretched.

He noticed that. I saw him looking at them.

And even though he was making eye contact with everyone but me, he was looking at me all covertly.

Jesus, Aria. You're imagining things. What the hell would a successful businessman like North see in a stupid high-school girl like you?

Get a grip.

"To be honest, Mr. North," Mrs. Chi says, "we're worried about the noise."

I already know that half the board thinks allowing North to buy a space is a bad idea. He's a developer, I've learned. Trying to gentrify the neighborhood by buying up properties on the cheap so he can renovate and sell at a premium.

"I have a solution for that," North says, making eye contact with everyone *but* me. "I'll only play at night. Say, nine PM to"—he shrugs—"two AM? That way I won't bother anyone during the day."

"We wouldn't want to restrict you like that," Mr. Garcia says. "It's not fair."

"Oh, it's no big deal," North says. "I work during the day. And I barely sleep. I get up at five AM every morning even though I don't have to be at work until nine. I figure staying up late pounding on the kit will help me develop better sleep habits. Tire me out, so to speak."

And then he does look at me. And is that a wink?

Mr. Garcia smiles his tight smile that says, *I'm not convinced*. But Mrs. Chi says, "If you'll excuse us now, we'll take a vote and let you know."

"Can I wait?" North asks. "I'd prefer to know before I leave, if that's OK."

"You may," Mrs. Chi says.

North stands up, thanking everyone politely, and then buttons his suit coat as he walks out.

Damn. The man is hot. Like, he's seriously old. Probably over thirty, but he's still very hot. His hair is kinda wild, for one thing. And he reached for a glass of water while everyone was talking and I think I glimpsed a tattoo under his shirt cuff.

21

Maybe he really is a drummer? Like some weird hybrid land developer by day and rock star at night?

"All those in favor?" Mr. Garcia is asking, not even pretending he's interested in having more debate. These people have really made up their mind, I guess.

Sucks to be you, Mr. Hot Drummer. They hate the idea.

When I look around I see that four of the board members have their hands up indicating yes. We should let him in. And four, including me, have hands on the table.

But just as Garcia opens his mouth to declare the motion denied, I raise my hand.

I don't know why I do it. April didn't have an opinion one way or the other. She barely mentioned tonight's agenda to me.

But that tattoo under his shirt cuff.

So sexy.

"Miss Amherst?" Mr. Garcia questions my decision. "Are you sure?"

I swallow hard and nod. "Yes. April told me to vote yes."

Lies, Aria. Nice start to your new life as an adult.

"Very well, then." Mr. Garcia sighs. "Motion to accept Mr. North's application has been accepted."

Everyone stands up, bustling around and gathering up papers. Mr. Garcia comes over to me as several of the yes voters exit, probably eager to talk to the sexy Mr. North and let him know the good news. "I'm very surprised that April told you to vote yes, Aria."

"Oh?" I say, my face heating up with embarrassment over my lie.

"I talked to her this morning and she said she had no opinion on the matter."

"Yes, well… she kinda said it on her way out this afternoon. Spur-of-the-moment reconsideration, maybe?" I smile.

Don't blush, don't blush, don't blush.

I blush.

"It's OK," Mr. Garcia says, patting my arm. "I didn't mean to upset you."

"I'm not upset," I say, feeling the heat on my cheeks.

"It's very sweet," he says.

"What is?" I ask.

"You're so young and innocent. But a breath of fresh air too. I will let Mr. North know you were the deciding vote."

I grab his arm to stop him, but he slips out of reach and heads for the door.

I follow, anxious that he will be talking about me to that hot, sexy, old guy with peekaboo tattoos under his expensive shirt cuff.

But I don't follow him out of the board room, just kind of hide behind the door frame. Which really doesn't hide me, because well, everything in this place is glass. So I only look stupid when Mr. Garcia goes up to North and shakes his hand, then points to me hiding behind nothing.

My face goes completely hot and my natural shyness takes over as I try to pretend that this sliver of steel door frame can actually hide my whole body if I look directly at it with my eyes so I can't see them.

I just stand there, shaking my head at my own childish stupidity.

"Thank you," North's rough, deep voice says.

I peek out from behind the frame and say, "What? Oh. No. Well… I didn't see you there." And then, because that was a disastrous incoherent babbling first impression, "Hey, no problem. I like drummers. We should all aspire to drum ourselves to sleep at night."

For fuck's sake, Aria.

He laughs. And, oh, wow, that laugh. Deep and rumbly. So much bass.

Then he touches me on the forearm, then pulls back quickly, like that was inappropriate, and I notice everyone else from the meeting is now pushing their way out of the front door.

I quickly glance around to find all the offices empty, and all the lights off except for the ballet dancer Jenna, who is frantically leaping and pirouetting or whatever the hell she's doing as classical music leaks out from behind her glass walls.

I'm practically alone with him.

"You do, huh?"

"What?" What did I say? I don't remember.

"Like drummers?" he helps.

"Oh, well… sure. Doesn't everyone?"

"No." He laughs. "No. I'd say our likability is right up there with tuba players."

"Tuba players." I almost snort. "That's funny. Every mother's nightmare, right?"

"Yes," he says, nodding his head. Smiling at me. And not the way he was smiling at everyone else, either. But the way he might smile at April.

"So you're Miss Amherst?" he says. "Owner's daughter."

"Yes, that's me. Miss Aria Amherst."

"Which studio is yours?" he asks.

"Oh, it's not—" But I stop. Because I realize he knows who I am, but yet he doesn't. He thinks I'm April. "It's... not anything special. Just that cube down there. Third on the left. And yours is..." I find the empty one. "There. Three down and on the opposite side from... mine."

Mine.

"Miss Amherst," he says, leaning his head down a little down as he inches closer to me. "Would you like to have a drink with me?"

"No," I say. Which makes him laugh. "I mean, no. I mean... no, but..." Jesus. I am so high-school right now. And he thinks I'm April. He thinks I'm some burgeoning photographer who needs a studio and is old enough to drink. Hell, old enough to be talking to him.

"No, but?" he prods. "You'll take a raincheck? Or you'd like to have a coffee instead? Or—"

26

"Yes," I say, brightening at his clever new offer. "Coffee! I can drink coffee."

He laughs again. "OK. Then coffee it is. What's good around here?"

"Nothing," I say.

"Aria." He laughs. "You're killing me. This neighborhood is amazing. They have lots of great coffee shops."

True. But they also know me. I come around here all the time with my family. And being seen alone with this man on a Friday night is just... hard nope.

"I mean, I'm tired of the Gingerbread, ya know? I live here"—God, saying that feels fantastic—"and work here, and you know, I like going other places."

"You live around here?" he asks.

"Mmm-hmm. Yup. Just about two blocks over."

He touches my face. Kinda caressing my cheek with the back of his knuckles. And suddenly I'm overwhelmed with feelings I've never felt before. Swoony feelings, and hot feelings, and throbby feelings.

"We could go there," he offers.

And then I make a mistake. A very big mistake. I look up into his eyes and die a little. Die with the fantasy of

27

taking a man—an older man. A much older man. Dressed up in a suit with a tie and actual cufflinks hiding peekaboo tattoos, and a drum set, or kit, or whatever you call it, waiting to be moved in to a cube down the hall from me to lead a secret drummer life at night, and—"OK," comes out of my mouth.

"OK," he says. "Lead on."

CHAPTER FOUR

She chats as we walk through the neighborhood. In fact, she never stops talking so I don't have to say anything. She rattles off facts about the various restaurants and shops, telling me what's good, or who sells what as we pass by. And I just get to look down at her small, petite body dressed up in that outfit that was clearly put together to drive men crazy.

When she stood up from the table and I realized she was wearing a black mini skirt with red sneakers—I chuckle as I look down at her feet—I wanted to bend her over the table in front of the entire board and take her from behind.

She is that fucking cute. Just plain adorable.

And she was the deciding vote. Garcia said it was close and if Miss Amherst hadn't have voted yes, I would've been denied. So I should tell her thank you.

And oh, I plan on it. I plan on thanking her very much.

Then the way she teased me as she stood in the doorway. Peeking out at me like she was some sexy little secret I needed to figure out.

She won't have a drink with me, and she won't go for coffee in public, but she'll take me back to her place.

Aria Amherst, you are a dream come true. The perfect one-night—

Oh, shit.

I can't one-night-stand this girl! I have to see her—

No. Hold up. I do not have to see her. I won't see her at all. I won't see anyone, that was the whole point of offering up night hours only in the co-op.

So… maybe I *can* one-night-stand this sweet little thing.

"OK, well, here we are," she says, stopping in front of her place. It's a three-story Victorian that has been clearly refurbished in the past few years. "I'm on top."

I chuckle at her innuendo.

"Oh." She blushes. "No," she says, waving a hand in front of her face. "I mean, top floor."

"Your mind is in the gutter this evening, Miss Amherst."

"Really." She blushes again.

It's so cute I can't take it. I take her hand, walk her up to the porch, and say, "Take me upstairs."

"Right," she says, pulling her hand out of mine so she can fish for her keys inside a little purse on a long strap. She finds them, unlocks the door, and waves me in.

"Oh, no. After you, sweet thing."

She exhales, a short burst of breath that lets me know she liked the term of endearment, and then begins walking up the stairs. Shooting me a nervous look over her shoulder every few steps as I try my best to hide the fact that I'm totally looking up her skirt at her creamy thighs and pink underwear.

CHAPTER FIVE

It occurs to me, when I get to the top of the stairs, that he might think this was an invitation for something other than coffee at my place.

Then I think, *Aria, you are so stupid.*

Of course he does! He's like forty or something! This man has probably been going home with women as long as I've been alive!

So then I get nervous and I can't find my key. I fumble with them. Then when I do have the right key, I can't seem to get it in the lock. And then when I do get it in the lock, the doorknob won't turn because this door is old, and weird, and—

"Here," he says, pushing his body close to mine. "Let me help you."

I back away, bumping into his chest as he reaches past me, brushing his arm against mine, and turns the handle to swing the door open.

I take a deep breath and hold it. Then walk forward so he can't hear me exhale, flick on the lights, and say, with all the control I can muster up, "Thanks."

"No problem," he says, closing the door behind him.

I set my purse and keys down on the small dining room table and turn to look at him. What the hell am I doing in my sister's apartment alone with this man? One day. I've been here one day and—

Felix meows, rubbing his body up against my legs. I bend down to pet him to take my mind off the fact that this guy now thinks I've invited him over for sex.

"So…" North says. "This is nice. How long have you lived here?"

"Um… four and half years," I say. Because that's how long April has lived here.

"Really?" he asks, raising his eyebrows. "How old are you?"

"Me?" I laugh nervously. "I'm twenty-five, why?"

He shakes his head. "No way."

"What do you mean, no way? I am. People always think I'm younger and I get carded all the time. I hate it."

April says this kind of stuff because she has a young look to her as well. So I'm just… channeling my older sister, I guess. When in Rome, you Rome.

Or something.

"You are so sweet, Aria. I swear to God, when you hit thirty you're gonna thank the gods for blessing you with youth."

I smile. Because that was nice. And if I really was twenty-five I'd probably want to hear something like that to make myself feel better about being old.

Especially coming out of this handsome man's mouth.

"How old are you?" I ask.

"How old do you think?"

"Mmmm… forty?"

"Forty?" He laughs.

"I mean, I can tell you're over thirty, but… I dunno. Everyone looks the same to me after that."

"What?" He chuckles again. "You're killing me, Aria."

He walks forward, closing the distance between us, but I whirl around and walk into the kitchen. He follows me halfway, leaning against the half wall that separates us.

"So... coffee?" I ask. Then I squint at the old fashioned coffee maker April uses. Oops. I forgot. She has one of those French presses. Which I don't know how to use because we have a real coffee maker at home that just requires you put a cup under the spout.

"Forget the coffee," I say, opening up the fridge. I'm just about to reach for bottled water when he leans in past me—how did he get behind me so fast?—and pulls out a bottle of wine.

"This'll do," he says. "Got a corkscrew?"

"I'm sure I do." I laugh, then look at the drawers. I've seen a corkscrew. I know she has one, but where would it live?

I pull open the silverware drawer and yes, there it is.

"Here you go," I say, thanking my lucky stars that I don't have to try to actually use it. Because I have no clue.

He pops the cork while I try to remember where she keeps her wine glasses. Luck is with me tonight, because they are on the second shelf in the same cupboard where the drinking glasses are.

"Here," he says, when I stand on my tiptoes trying to reach them. "I've got it."

"I'm not much of an entertainer, am I?" I say.

"No bother," he says, pouring us both wine.

36

I don't drink wine except on special occasions with my parents. Christmas and holidays, stuff like that. But I think I can pull this off.

"Cheers," I say.

He smiles and says, "To meeting you. I thought for sure this night was gonna be awful, but this... *this* makes up for that board meeting."

"Awkward." I laugh, then realize I sound like a teenager. "I mean, I'm glad it worked out for you."

"Oh, it's working out," he says, taking a sip of his wine and putting it down. "Now what should we do?"

Jesus. Is this how one-night stands go? Do people discuss things beforehand? Because my only experience with a one-night stand is with Lawrence Ballenshine at summer camp two years ago. And even though I tell people I had sex with him, I'm not really sure he actually put it in. I just know it kinda hurt and then there was sticky white come all over my legs.

My point is, Larry and I didn't talk about it. There was no, *What now?* He just started groping me behind a tree and I groped him back, and then... sticky white come.

"Um... so what do you do, Mr. North?"

"Mr. North," he says. "That's cute. You can call me Ryker, if you want."

37

Ryker. Holy shit. That's hot. "OK, Ryker," I say, feeling the back of my neck prickle with heat again.

He shakes his head at me, probably because I'm blushing and guys like that, right? "I'm a real-estate developer."

"Oh, I did hear that," I say, trying to make myself act normal. "They were talking about it in the meeting before you got there."

"Yeah, well. We get a bad rep. But we're not all evil."

"Are you one of the good ones, then?"

He nods, then taking a step and closing the short distance between us. "I am," he says, taking my glass and setting it down. "And you are very, very pretty, Aria."

He does that knuckle thing across my cheek again and I die a little inside. That throbby thing starts happening between my legs, my skin flushing as my hands get all sweaty.

Please don't take my hand.

He takes my hand. "Am I making you nervous?" he asks. "Your palms are all sweaty and your face is all red."

"I'm sorry," I say. "It's just... this is just so... and I don't normally... and yes," I admit. "You are. I really didn't mean to imply anything when I asked you over. I'm just…"

"Very"—he lifts my hand to his mouth and kisses my fingers—"very"—he kisses them again—"sweet."

"Yes," I say, nodding. "Yes. That's right. I'm sweet."

As in inexperienced. Because I have no idea what to do right now and I really think he needs to just leave. And I don't know how to say that except… "I think you should leave."

"What?" He laughs.

"I'm sorry. I just have an early morning tomorrow and… well, I have to go to bed now."

He glances at the clock on the wall. "It's eight o'clock."

"I know, early, right? Early to bed, early to rise—"

"Are you OK?"

"Fine. So fine. Better than fine. I'm great. And you're great. And sexy." I giggle. "Too sexy, I think. Way too sexy. And older. So…"

He looks at me pointedly. "You're not twenty-five, are you?"

I nod my head yes, but at the same time I say, "No. I lied. I'm seventeen. I'm sorry! This is my sister's apartment and I'm cat-feeding and school-going, and I'm just in her studio to do a Photoshop class!"

"Holy fuck," he says, working his jaw a little.

"I'm really sorry. I'm so, so sorry. I didn't mean to lie! I swear. I just—"

And then he kisses me. He takes my face in his hands, and leans down, and opens his mouth and sticks his tongue right inside me.

And I'm not sure what to do except the same.

Because Larry and I didn't do much kissing back behind that tree at summer camp and the only other boy I've kissed is Matt Manning at the Valentine's Day dance last month and he did not open his mouth or stick his tongue inside me.

So that's it. My only option is to do to him exactly what he's doing to me.

"When will you turn eighteen?" he whispers into my mouth.

"Sunday," I whisper back.

"Two days from now?" he asks, still kissing me.

"Mmmm-hmmm," I mumble back, thinking if this is kissing I should've started doing it sooner.

He pulls away, a pained look on his face. I know he's going to leave. Right now. He's going to yell at me for deceiving him and walk right out my sister's door.

"Oh, God, Aria."

"I'm so sorry. I really am. I won't tell anyone if you don't. Please don't tell anyone I brought you up here. My father would be pissed and he'll drag me home to the boring suburbs, and my exciting pretend adult life in the city will be over!"

He exhales.

"You're mad," I say. "I know you're mad. And… and I'm bad. I know that. This was bad. I'm bad. And I probably deserve to go home."

"No," he says. "That's not what I'm thinking about right now."

"You're not?" I say, genuinely surprised because if I were him, I'd be thinking that yeah, this girl has no clue what she's doing and has no business being left alone in her sister's apartment in the city for four weeks.

But thank God, I don't say any of that out loud. Instead, I say, "Then what are you thinking about?"

He looks at me hungrily. Like he's the Big Bad Wolf and I'm Little Red. Like he wants to eat me up in one gulp.

And I look back at him like maybe I want him to do that.

"Two days?" he asks again.

"Yes." I nod. "I'm meeting my parents for tea at the Corinthian and then we're going to see that musical everyone's talking about."

"God help me," he says.

"What? Why? I said I was sorry. Please don't tell. *Please*," I beg.

"I'm not gonna tell, Aria."

"You're not?" I brighten.

"Not if you don't," he says. And that hungry look is back. Only it's like he's starving and needs to eat something *now*. Anything, even if it's me.

And to tell the truth, I feel the same way. My body is all tingly and my lips—I reach up to touch them. They feel all weird. His touch lingering. The minty taste of his mouth still fresh inside mine.

"What are you thinking about?" I ask.

He reaches for me, then steps back without touching. I want him to touch me, I realize. I didn't intend for that to happen when I brought him up here, but I do.

But I see that he's about to leave, to walk out and never come back, so I reach for him.

He shakes his head and backs away. "I shouldn't have kissed you. I just can't..."

I wait for him to continue, but he doesn't. So I say, "You can't what?"

"I can't help myself. I have to go before I do something stupid."

"No!" I say, grabbing onto the sleeve of his coat. "Just... wait."

He looks at me over his shoulder and says, "Aria. If I stay here another second I'm going to lift up your little skirt, pull down your pink panties, and stick my fingers inside you until you come."

My mouth drops open.

"And if you open your mouth like that again, I'll stick my cock inside it."

I shut my mouth.

"I'm sorry," he says, shaking his head. "That was so fucking inappropriate."

Which it totally was. But it was also totally hot.

"I gotta go."

43

And then he does. He leaves. He opens the door, walks through it in a rush, and closes it behind him.

And when I open it back up to call him back, he's already out of sight. Nothing but footsteps on the stairs.

I close the door and lean against it, totally breathing hard and my mind a whirlwind of thoughts.

Mostly thoughts of him bending me over, lifting up my little skirt, pulling my pink panties down, and sticking his fingers inside me.

And I know I said I wasn't going to use my sister's toys but I'm already walking to the bathroom where she keeps them all.

I bend down in front of the vanity, wondering how he knew my panties were pink, then realize I walked up the stairs in front of him and gave him a peek up three whole flights—and stop.

"What the hell is this?"

I reach into the basket of sex toys and pull out a box with a note on it that says *Aria* in thick, black Sharpie.

"'Because I know it's temping and you are not allowed to use my toys,'" I say, reading her note. It's a brand-new vibrator still in the package.

I slump down on the floor, my fingers so eager to open the package I end up just ripping the top of the box off, and pull out the bright pink vibrator along with the batteries.

Thirty seconds later the batteries are in and I turn it on, stare at it for a second as it hums and vibrates, then reach between my legs with one hand, pull my pink panties aside, and close my eyes so I can pretend Ryker is doing this to me. Then, with the other hand, I place the tip of the vibrator up to my clit.

"Holy shit," I moan. "Holy fucking shit! Why didn't I buy one of these years ago?"

I don't last much longer than that one sentence. I can't help it. It's my first time. And my first time feels… spectacular.

And a few seconds later, it's all over.

That hot feeling is gone, the unquenchable desire quenched.

But Ryker's face lingers in my mind. His angled jaw that felt a little like sandpaper when he kissed me. And the kissing. His tongue. His… threats if he stayed any longer.

"Ryker," I whisper, lowering the still-vibrating vibrator down between my legs again. "Ryker," I say again, closing my eyes.

It takes a little longer this time, but that's OK. And when I'm done I strip off all my clothes and take the vibrator to bed with me.

CHAPTER SIX

"Seventeen," *I say*, over and over again as I walk back to the co-op. When I get there I realize my driver dropped me off because I said I'd call him when I was done so he didn't have to wait in the parking lot.

Which I do. Call him, I mean. Still muttering, "Seven-fucking-teen," as he answers the phone.

"Mr. North. What was that?"

"Can you come pick me up?" I ask.

"Be right there, sir."

I end the call and loiter out in front of the building, hands in my pockets because I don't know what to do with them.

Seventeen.

And it doesn't even matter that she'll be eighteen in two days because even eighteen is too damn young.

Hell, twenty-five is too young. I'm thirty-five. Even if she was her sister, I'd have almost nothing in common with her. I've done this enough to know that it's pointless. Younger women are just more trouble than they're worth when you're my age. They are exploring, they are testing limits, they are going places. Always going places.

Which… fine. I'm not even interested in a relationship. It's never anything more than one night. And besides, I just have a thing for them. I don't know why I'm attracted to the young ones, I just am.

But this… "No," I caution myself. "No, no, no."

This is a very big mistake waiting to happen. Because at twenty-five, most of these girls understand what I'm doing.

Which is using them. But most of them are using me too.

Not all of them. But most of them.

Some of them are like Aria, though not that young. Hell, I've never dipped that low before. But some of them are sweet like her and not dirty. They have romantic ideas, and expectations, and are shy, but eager.

Those are the best ones.

48

Shy and eager.

And with these girls I always have to explain to them it's just sex. I make sure they understand.

Seventeen... they don't get that. Not even at eighteen. Two days. I laugh. Two days makes no difference at all. At seventeen their minds are filled with what-ifs and possibilities.

I've fucked them as young as twenty before and even that's a mistake.

So seventeen is just no.

Put her out of your head. Pretend this night never happened. Just... forget about her.

But I can't. God, I can't. I picture myself doing things to her. The exact things I said I'd do. Lifting up her little skirt, pulling her panties down to her knees and leaving them there as I finger her to climax with her face pushed up against a wall.

And by the time my driver pulls up a few minutes later, I'm hard.

I get in the back seat trying to adjust my cock so it can spread out along my leg underneath my slacks.

I want to jack off to the image of her sweet, sweet face moaning and twisting as I make her come with my fingers.

49

"Home?" the driver asks. "Or somewhere else tonight, Mr. North?"

It's too early for me to go home. I don't usually go home until late on workdays. And on Friday nights I go to bars, or restaurants, or the fake apartments of little girls.

Stop it, I warn myself.

You are not going to fuck this girl. Not even on Sunday when she turns eighteen.

You are going out tonight. You're going to pick up some random woman, take her home, or go to her place, fuck her brains out while not thinking about Aria Amherst's pink panties, and you're going to get rid of this hard-on and never think about what just happened again.

"Mr. North?"

"Yes," I say. "Take me home."

Because I need to jerk off to those pink panties before the memory fades.

When I get up to my penthouse apartment uptown my hard-on is still raging. I take off my jacket, throw it on a chair, and unbuckle my belt as I walk towards the couch and take a seat.

Two seconds later my cock is in my fist and I'm jerking off as I picture what it would be like to be inside her sweet pussy.

"Aria," I mutter, pumping my cock. "What are you doing to me?"

I close my eyes and picture the way her tits pressed against her button-down shirt. Imagine myself ripping her buttons off and pulling her shirt aside to reveal a pink bra that matches her panties. Then pulling that down so her breasts lift up and her nipples perk out.

Then I'm gonna sink my mouth down over her nipples, and play with her pussy until her underwear is all wet, and then...

I come. All over my slacks.

And I realize that it wasn't a fantasy.

It was a plan.

I wake in the morning to the sound of my phone ringing.

"Hello?" I ask, my voice rough and deep from sleep. I was up for hours jerking off to the memory of sweet, young Aria. I don't think I've jerked off that many times in one night since I was fourteen.

51

"Mr. North? This is Mr. Garcia at the co-op?"

"Yes," I say, forcing myself to concentrate.

"We have another interested party and we're eager to sell this unit, so if you could get your loan—"

"I'll be there in an hour with cash."

"Oh," he says. "OK. Very well. I'll get the paperwork ready."

"Thank you," I say, and end the call.

I'm not going in so I can see her.

I'm not.

And it turns out I'm not. Because she's not there. Everyone else is there. Apparently Saturday mornings are when the artists come out. Because every glass cube is busy... except one.

Aria's. Which is three down from mine and on the opposite side of the hall.

I peek into it as I walk by, trying to get a glimpse of what goes on in there. It's her sister's, I get that. But she said she was using it for Photoshop or something.

52

"Right this way," Garcia says, panning his hand into the board room.

And an hour later, I've sent a hundred and ninety-five thousand dollars to the co-op account and he's handing me the keys.

"Nine PM to two AM," he reminds me.

"Got it," I say.

"Welcome to the co-op, Mr. North. I hope your time here is satisfying."

"Thank you," I say, then meander down to my cube and open it up.

There's some shelves on the wall, but that's it. The last person in here was another musician, so it's just empty space now.

"When do you think you'll be moving in?" Garcia asks from the hallway.

"Tomorrow night," I say. Because it's Aria Amherst's birthday and I have a big, fat cock as her present.

"Very good," he says. And I almost laugh. If he only knew what I was thinking. "I'll let everyone know that if they want to work at night they can't complain about the drums."

"Appreciate it," I say. "And thanks again. I think my time here at the co-op is gonna be... fun."

Ozzy calls later that day asking if I want to go to a club with him and some girls he met last night, but I tell him no. I have to get my drum kit ready for moving.

But I don't do that. It's not even set up in my apartment. It's down in my storage locker in a huge castor-wheeled case. So all I have to do is roll it out to the movers I hired.

I think about her. I don't want to think about her. Young women have been a weakness of mine ever since I turned thirty. I get it. Classic recapturing of my youth and all that bullshit.

But that's not it. I don't feel old and thirty-five isn't old, anyway. It's not me, it's them.

Especially sweet ones like Aria. Innocent ones. Is she a virgin?

God, that would be like winning the lottery.

But it doesn't even matter if she's not. She's new, and shiny, and malleable.

I bet her blow jobs are terrible. I bet she thinks fucking is missionary position. I bet she's never even watched porn.

I want to corrupt her.

That's my sick reason for liking them young.

I want to corrupt them.

I want to take all that sweetness inside them and soil it. Turn them dirty. Turn them from shy and inexperienced into cock-sucking experts by the end of the night.

I'm doing all their future boyfriends a service.

OK. I get it. Ryker North is an asshole. A giant, selfish dick who wants nothing to do with feelings, or negotiations, or plans for the future.

But she's seventeen, not twenty-five.

Which might be a good thing. Because her plans have nothing to do with marriage, or ticking clocks, or houses in the suburbs. That's why my cut-off is twenty-five. Any older than that and the word 'relationship' pops up after the third date.

Hell, her plans right now are probably all about final exams, and backpacking through Europe over the summer, and starting college in the fall.

So maybe that's a good thing?

Do I hear myself right now? I'm trying to justify wanting to fuck an eighteen-year-old girl because she has teenage expectations instead of twenty-something aspirations on her mind?

So I'm an asshole.

I decide to just own that shit before I go down to the garage, get in my car, drive over to the co-op, and park in the back lot.

I own that shit before I walk inside looking for her. Before I walk the two blocks over to her house and stare up at her window while I hide in the shadows across the street.

But after I see her walking across the living room, I become more than an asshole.

I become something more along the lines of... a predator.

Because I'm gonna do it. There's just no way I can't. I'm gonna make sure I see her again so I can do all those things I fantasized about last night.

Maybe even more than once.

CHAPTER SEVEN

I wake up on Sunday feeling no different than I did last night.

But you're eighteen, Aria!

Hmmmm... nope. No different. Two nights. I've been here two nights and the only place I've gone is the co-op—secretly hoping to bump into Ryker, even though I'm pretty sure he never wants to see my face again—and the burger place half a block down on State Street.

I chatted with friends online and grammed my new place. But everybody knows I'm just cat-sitting for my sister and no one is impressed.

Ryker's name never comes up in those convos. In fact, even though he got me all hot that night, the vibrator did the trick for me. Inviting him over was a stupid thing to do. I have a class starting on Monday. I'm going to meet college boys. I might even like one and go on coffee dates.

I'm pretty sure that's gonna happen. I can feel it. Something exciting is gonna come out of this little city vacation and then when I get back to school in two weeks I'll have all kinds of amazing stories to tell my friends and hey, maybe I'll even keep in touch with that boy I know I'm gonna meet on campus tomorrow.

But the main thing is... I'm gonna have stories to tell in school. So maybe I won't spend the last few weeks of high school being the smart, quiet girl who sits in front for every single class and never goes anywhere on the weekends except home or out with her parents. Maybe I'll be that girl who stayed at her sister's apartment in the city for two weeks and went all crazy and wild.

I walk into the lobby of the Corinthian Hotel still smiling about that. It's ridiculous, I know. But this is what all not-so-popular girls dream about in their senior year. To be somebody people admire and want to hang out with.

My father is holding balloons and my mother is holding a small gift.

"Hi, Mom and Dad!" I say brightly.

"Happy birthday, honey! How was your weekend?" my mother asks. She's very pretty for a mom. She's only forty-two and she was just my age when she had my sister. It was totally a shotgun wedding, but no one cared because my father's family is super-rich and her family wasn't, so it's kind of a miracle they're still together. "Did you do anything exciting?" she asks.

"Nope," I say. "Just hung out with Felix and ordered a burger from down the block."

"You have to get out more, honey," my mom says, tucking a piece of hair behind my ear.

Which I hate, so I swipe her hand away while my father says, "Leave her alone, Doris. She's not into socializing."

And he means well, but it kinda hurts. I would like to be outgoing and put myself out there. I would like to be a socializer. I'm just… not.

My father is older than her by fourteen years. Which is something I don't think about much except… Ryker. That reminds me of him and how he's practically old enough to be my father.

OMG. What if he's the same age as my mom?

I giggle to myself, then play it off like I'm excited about the balloons and the gift as we're led to our table for high tea.

I love high tea. And after this we're going to a show together. I love musicals. We used to go a lot because April was always in the theatre club in high school but kinda grew out of it since she left home.

After we're seated and we make our selections for tea and finger food, my mother hands me the gift. "Open it," she says.

Even though my parents are loaded we only get one gift for our birthday from the both of them, and then two each on Christmas. Which sounds stingy, but isn't, because their gifts are always huge.

Like April's apartment. She got that the first Christmas she was in college as a reward for getting straight A's that semester.

So I kinda know what I'm getting. A car, of course. And inside this little box is a key fob. And outside in the parking lot—or maybe waiting in the driveway at home, since my father probably wouldn't want me driving in the city—is a shiny car. Probably something practical, like a Volvo. But maybe, possibly it's a little convertible? Wouldn't that be amazing?

I'm so sure of this that I'm already squealing when I lift the lid off and find… "A diamond ring?" I say, lifting it out.

"It was your grandmother's. I know she'd want you to have it," my father says.

My grandma died last year so now I'm feeling guilty for expecting a car and getting a ring.

"It's so pretty," I say, trying to be gracious. I slide it on my finger and admire it. Because it is totally beautiful.

60

It's just… not a car.

"I love it," I say. And I do. Just not as much as I would a car.

"I'm so glad," my mom says. "I told your father we should get you a car, but he said this was more meaningful. Every kid gets a car when they're eighteen."

Which isn't true, obviously. Because April got one at sixteen when I got Space Camp.

But I rally and smile. "It's so perfect," I say, getting up from my seat so I can give them both a kiss. "I will love it and cherish it forever."

"If you'd prefer a car, Aria, we could—"

"No, no, no, Dad. *No.* This is just perfect. Thank you. So much. I love it. Best birthday ever." Because I am blushing with guilt for not being thankful enough. "I'm never going to take it off."

"Put in on your left hand, Aria. That way all the boys will think you're engaged at that college class next week and leave you alone."

"Dad," I fake-whine. "Stop it."

He smiles at me and then leans in to kiss my mother on the cheek. "We did good," he whispers to her.

I love that my parents are still in love. When everyone else I know is trading time between two households and getting used to stepparents and new babies, my family is rock solid.

So no. I am not going to complain about getting a diamond ring from my grandmother instead of a car. And I do put it on my left hand to make my father happy.

By the time the show is over and my birthday is winding down, it's nearly midnight and my parents are taking me home.

God, that's weird.

"What time is class tomorrow?" my mother asks.

"Not 'till eleven," I say.

"I'm going to miss you on the commute, Aria. It won't be the same without you."

"I know, Dad. But I'll be back in a month and then we can spend the last two weeks of the semester riding into the city. Oh," I say. "Can you stop by the co-op real fast? I have to pick up my flash drive for class tomorrow."

"Sure, honey," my mom says.

We pull around the corner and I'm surprised to see the lights on inside. The glass front is frosted and nearly opaque so we can't see who's inside when my dad pulls the car up to the door.

"Be right back," I say, getting out of the car, then realize the balloons my parents got me for my birthday are tied to my wrist. "Shit," I say, tugging on them to get them off.

"Language," my mother says, softly.

I let the balloons stay. I'll just be a second, anyway. When I get inside there is one cube light on.

Ryker North's.

He's bending down doing something with his drums when I go to my cube and unlock it.

I'm staring at him over my shoulder when he looks up. "Hmmm," he says.

I turn away and go into my cube, grab my drive, and then lock back up.

He's standing in his doorway now, watching me.

He's wearing a pair of faded jeans and no shirt. And that peekaboo view of his tattoo I caught a glimpse of the other night—full view now.

Holy shit. His chest is like chiseled stone. Hard and smooth, and very, very muscular. There's a slight sheen

63

of sweat all over him and he's got full-sleeve tattoos running down his arms in black and red, and his hair is falling over into his face.

Is this the same guy? This cannot be the same guy. He looks nothing like the Ryker North I met on Friday. He looks… like a fucking drummer.

"Happy birthday," he says, leaning one hip against the door frame and crossing his arms. "I see you've been partying." He nods his chin to the heart-shaped Mylar balloons tied to my wrist.

"Thanks," I say, reaching up to twirl my hair. It's a nervous habit that I hate, and it jerks the balloons around like crazy, so I stop and shove my hands into my dress pockets.

His eyes track that movement. "What the fuck is that on your finger? Is that a… did you get engaged?"

"What?" Then I remember the ring. "Oh, this?" I say, bringing my hand out of my pocket so I can flash my diamond at him. Balloons bobbing in the air above my head. "Yup. I'm engaged." He furrows his brow so deeply I do that backward chin thing in surprise. "What? I'm joking. It was a birthday present from my father. It used to belong to my grandma."

His expression relaxes. "Oh."

"Wow," I say. "You had a very strange reaction to that."

He stares at me for a moment, then shakes his head and turns his back—and oh, Lord, it's just as delicious as the front. Two demons on each of his shoulder blades connected by some swirly, smoky design elements.

"I like your tattoos," I say. "They're pretty hot."

He looks at me over his shoulder as he bends down to do whatever to his drums, stretching his back muscles as he reaches forward. "I like your dress. You should take it off."

I blink at him. "What?" Then I laugh.

"Take it off. You're eighteen now. Legal." He winks.

"My mom and dad are outside in the car."

"Get rid of them."

"No," I say. "They're driving me home."

"I'll drive you home."

"OK, it was nice seeing you again, but you're way too old for me so I'm not…" I shake my head. "I'm not…"

I can't think what I'm not gonna do because he stands back up and walks over to me. Too close, actually. He puts both hands against the glass on either side of my head and leans down.

He smells like cologne, and man, and something else. Sweat maybe. Or is that sex?

"You're not gonna what?" he asks, looking at my lips. And I'm looking at his too. The way they purse a little when he says, *What?*

I duck under his arms and start walking to the front door. He's way too much for me. I mean, look at him.

I look at him over my shoulder as I near the door.

He's a man and I'm really still just a girl.

"Why are you running away from me, Aria?" he asks, following me to the door.

"I just gotta go. My parents are outside."

"Should I say hi to them?" he asks, coming too close to me again.

"No!" I laugh. "And get away from me. My father will see you."

"Can't see through the glass," he says, boxing me in again.

"He can see our shadows," I say, starting to get nervous.

"Kiss me," he says.

"No," I say. "I'm not getting involved with you. You're too old, and too…"

"Too what?"

"Too much, OK? You're way too much for me. I'm going to find a nice boy to date at class tomorrow and forget all about that kiss up in my sister's apartment."

"You sure about that, Aria?" I'm still watching his lips when he leans in.

Still very sure that this won't happen because I say, "I'm sure."

Except I say it just before his lips touch mine.

It's the same kind of kiss as it was on Friday. Open mouth, probing tongue, and then he grabs my hair with both hands and won't let me go.

He *makes* me kiss him.

Which is stupid and ridiculous because I kiss him back so hard. I swirl my tongue with his and then my hand goes to his waist and he sucks in a breath of air, so I pull it away real fast, unsure why I just did that.

The horn honks outside and he pulls back, smiling. Then he turns away and calls over his shoulder, "Tell your parents I said hi."

I huff, swiping my fingertips over my lips where he was just kissing them.

"And leave your door unlocked when you get home. I'm coming over."

"What?" I whisper.

"Oh," he says. "And don't change your clothes or take those balloons off your wrist. It's all part of my fantasy."

Oh, shit.

I turn away, open the door and run out, heart-shaped balloons bobbing wildly behind me as my own heart begins to stutter and thump in my chest.

"Was someone in there with you?" my father asks, once I'm buckled into the back seat and he's pulling away.

"Just that new guy," I say. I was gonna say Mrs. Chi or Mr. Garcia, but I'm sure my father could probably tell from the shadow it wasn't them. They are both on the short side and Ryker is massive.

Before he can ask any more awkward questions we arrive at my sister's house and I open the door, calling out, "Thanks for the great birthday! I'll see you soon!" and rush up to the house before they can stop me.

CHAPTER EIGHT

It's gonna be a one-night thing. I just want to get it over with. Just fuck her and leave. Then I never have to think about it again. It's done.

That's what I tell myself as I drive over to her apartment and park in the back lot. I planned this night. Every detail. Of course, I didn't know for sure that she'd come by the co-op, but I had a feeling. So I made sure to take off my shirt and I took my time setting up my drums, and sure enough, she showed.

If she didn't show I was gonna walk away. Just let it go and stop thinking about her. I really was.

But now that's off the table. I need to fuck this girl. She showed up in that little dress—white with pink flowers. And a thin, pink cardigan with little pearly buttons, and some fucking heart-shaped balloons tied to her goddamned wrist.

I get hard just thinking about it. I get so hard I have to reach inside my pants and shift my cock. Twice, this girl has done that to me. Twice in two days.

Yeah, I just need to get this over with.

I get out of the car and walk up to her porch. The buzzer is optional because the door doesn't lock. I checked it out last night when I came over to watch her. So I don't announce myself. Just go inside and climb up the three flights of stairs until I'm standing in front of her door, knuckles ready to knock, when I hesitate.

Last chance, Ryker.

Fuck that. And I don't knock, I try the doorknob and find it unlocked.

Oh, I will reward you for that, Miss Amherst.

I swing the door open and find her leaning against the kitchen counter on the other side of the half wall that separates her from the little dining area. Then I swing it closed and make a show of locking it behind me.

"What are you doing?" she asks.

I take off my leather jacket—must look the part tonight, right?—and drop it over the back of a chair as I walk towards her, entering the kitchen. She's got wide eyes, but she didn't change her dress and those fucking balloons are still tied to her wrist.

70

"I'm here to say happy birthday," I say, easing my body up to hers and sliding my hands around her waist as I press my hips into her stomach. She's tiny compared to me. "And bring you a present."

"What present?" she asks, looking up at me with those wide, innocent eyes.

I take her hand off the counter and place it over my hard cock. Make her squeeze it. "This," I say.

"I told you, I'm not getting involved with you."

"No, you're right. We're not getting involved, Aria." I smile down at her. "We're just going to fuck. One night, that's all. I don't do relationships, so don't worry about that. But you want me, I know you do. And I definitely want you. So…"

"So you think you can just come over here and… what? Use me?"

"We use each other, Aria. That's what grownups do."

"Fuck you," she says. "You don't get to tell me how to act."

"Is this when you tell me I'm not your daddy?"

She pushes on my chest and I take a step back. Which allows her to duck away and walk over to the living room.

"You kissed me back."

71

"You kissed me first!"

"You left your door unlocked and those balloons are still tied to your wrist. So come on now. Don't lie to me. If you want me to leave, tell me to leave and I'll go. I'll go and never come back. Never bother you again. But if you want this one chance to be properly fucked by a man who knows what he's doing and not some boy with a skinny little pecker from your Photoshop class, then..." I hold out my arms, palms up. "Then say yes. No strings, OK? Just this night, just this once and I'm gone."

"Why?" she says. "Why would you even want to bother with me?"

"Why?" I laugh. Too loud, maybe. But it's so ridiculous. "Because you look like *that.*"

She looks down at herself, then back up at me. "Like what?"

Jesus. She has no clue. This is why I like the younger ones. Especially ones like her. I walk over to her and take her hand. Kiss her knuckles and then place her palm over my cock. "Innocent," I say. "And unaware of how desirable that innocence is." I squeeze her hand over my cock and she blushes and looks down. "You're a sweet little thing, Aria. A very sweet thing."

She pulls her hand away, biting her lip and folding her arms across her chest. Which puts the balloons squarely between her and me. I grab each string and pull them apart. Just like I'm gonna pull open her legs tonight. And say, "Want me to teach you something?"

"Teach me what?" she asks, her voice quivering. "How to suck your cock?"

"Ohhhh," I say. "You have a dirty mouth. I love that, by the way. But no. It's your birthday, remember? You get a gift."

"Your cock," she says. And damn. She's killing me with that mouth.

"Before that," I say. "Before I give you my cock I'll teach you how to come."

"I know how to come," she sneers. "I get myself off all the time."

I raise an eyebrow at her. "Tell me more."

She laughs, shaking her head and hiding her face with her hand. "No."

"No, you don't want my gift? Or no, you don't want me at all? Because I need to know if I should stay or not."

"I don't know."

"Aria," I say, too sharply. "Stop fucking around and acting like a baby. Do you want me to lick your pussy tonight or not?"

She sucks in a deep breath.

"It's OK," I say. "You can tell me yes or no. Either way, I'm not judging you. If you say yes, I'll do it. I'll take you over to the couch, sit you down, spread your legs and eat you out until you come in my mouth. And if you say no, I'll just grab my jacket and leave. Never come back again."

She looks like she might cry so I reach for her wrist and start removing her balloon strings. She lets me without saying a word, but when I let the balloons go and they float up to the high ceiling, there's nothing left for her to hide behind.

"Time to make a decision," I say. "Want your present or not?"

She swallows hard and nods her head.

I shake mine. "You gotta say the word, Aria. It's important that I have your permission, but even more important that I hear you say yes so I can jerk off to your scared little face as you give in to me for the rest of my life."

"That's gross!"

"Yeah, well. I'm pretty sure every man who saw you tonight is jerking off to your face right now." I pause at that thought. Because I just kind of said it without thinking. "And actually," I amend, "that is gross. No one gets to jerk off to you except me."

She cracks a smile and inhales deeply. "Yes," she says, quietly. Then she looks up at me. Locks her eyes right on mine and says it again. "Yes. I want you to give me my birthday present."

I feel fifteen again. Like I'm gonna blow a load in my pants. That's how hot she is right now. That's how turned on I am.

"Good choice," I whisper, taking her hand and leading her over to the couch. "Now sit down and spread your legs."

"Oh, God," she mutters, fingers splayed over her face in embarrassment.

Which just about kills me dead.

But she does it. She sits down, prim and proper. Just her butt cheeks on the edge of the couch. Then she places both hands on the cushions and scoots all the way back.

She looks up at me. Maybe for validation or maybe with hesitation, but it doesn't matter which, because my nodding head is just the encouragement she needs. Because she closes her eyes and opens her legs.

The skirt of her dress is longer than the mini she was wearing the first night. So I can't see her panties or even her upper thighs. It's also much looser. A full skirt with large pink flowers scattered all over it.

I take off my shirt, and the movement makes her open her eyes. She stares at my bare chest. Not hungrily, the way I look at her. But with something akin to awe.

I kneel down between her legs and place my hands on her knees, opening them wider. She sucks in a breath of air and lets it out with a tiny whimper.

God, I really like that sound.

"Scoot down a little," I say, grabbing her behind the knees and pulling. She does, until her ass cheeks are hanging over the edge. And that's when I push her skirt up and see her pink panties. They are silky, but not overly sexy. Like she shops in the juniors department and not at Victoria's Secret.

I love them. I love them so much I lean my head forward and kiss them.

I can feel her pussy lips beneath the thin fabric and my tongue darts out and licks her.

"Should I take them off?" she asks.

I look up at her. Her tits are rising and falling quickly, indicating she's breathing harder now. "No," I say. "I like them on."

"But you can't—"

"Aria," I say. "Men don't care if they have to work around your panties. We like it."

"Why?"

"Because…" I think about this for a minute. "Because it feels like we're taking something from you. Sneaking it. If we fuck you and you still have clothes on it's hot because we're so desperate to fuck you, we can't be bothered to take them off."

"Oh," she says. "But they're getting wet."

"We like that too," I say. "Now close your eyes and think about my mouth. And because you asked so many questions about it, I'm going to make you come through your panties so you know I'm not lying."

"Oh," she gasps.

I lean my head in again and swipe my tongue along her slit. My hands pressing her thighs open. My thumbs caressing small circles over her smooth skin. She arches her back when I hit her clit and when my finger parts her pussy open though her silky panties, she begins to groan.

God, she's primed and ready. My cock is throbbing in my jeans.

"Has anyone ever eaten you out before?" I ask her, still licking.

"No," she moans. Shaking her head.

"Do you like it?"

"Yes," she squeaks, because I nipped her panties and got a bit of skin too.

"Then put your hands on my head, Aria. And grip my hair."

She reaches for me. Tentatively placing her hands on my head and threading her fingers into my hair.

"Grip it hard," I say. "And if you think I'm not in the right place, guide me. Tell me where you want me to lick you."

"Oh, my God," she moans.

"Do it," I say, licking her all around her clit, but not directly on her clit. Because I want to feel her hands guiding me. I want to know she's participating.

She doesn't do that though. So I give her a little help. "Right here?" I ask, licking her in the wrong place.

"No," she says.

"Then show me. Show me where I should lick you, Aria. Show me with your hands."

She reaches down, pulls her panties aside, and begins to massage her clit.

Jesus Christ. I meant guide my mouth to it, but hell, this is better.

"Oh, you're a dirty girl," I say, placing my lips over her finger and flicking my tongue against her sweet, little nub.

"Yes," she moans. "Right there."

She arches her back again, her legs going stiff as she presses them against my head.

I grab her knees and spread her open again as she writhes and wiggles on the couch so much, she almost slides off completely.

"Come for me, sweet thing," I say, easing my finger up inside her a little.

"Ow," she says.

Which makes me stop and raise my eyebrows.

"I'm OK," she says. "Don't stop."

Holy shit, is she a virgin? One finger and she's gasping in pain? I ease my finger up a little more and she hisses through her teeth, her hands gripping my head now, but not to guide me, to push me away.

"Aria?" I say. "Are you all right?"

"Yes," she says, out of breath. "It just hurts a little."

"Are you a virgin?"

"I don't think so," she moans.

I take my finger out of her and sit back. "Hold on," I say. "You don't *think so*?"

She opens her eyes and nods. "I had sex once, I think."

"You think? Aria, you either did or didn't. Which is it?"

"I think I did," she says. "He came all over me."

"He came... but not inside you."

"No, he came on my hand."

"So you gave him a hand job?"

"I guess."

"Did he put his little pecker inside you?"

"I think so."

I shake my head at her. "No," I say. "No, it doesn't work that way, Aria. You'd know. For sure."

"I think he was inside me, but maybe not all the way."

"Do you want me to check?"

"Check what?"

I laugh. This is the most absurd conversation I've ever had with a girl... *ever*. "To see if he popped your cherry."

"You can see that?"

"Yeah," I say.

"You've done this before?"

"Not check hymens!" I laugh. "Take someone's virginity, yes. Couple times when I was younger. Not in a long while, though."

She bites her lip then nods her head. "Yes. Then check to see."

"OK," I say. "But let me take your panties down, all right?"

"OK," she says.

I pull at the waistband and she lifts her hips, allowing me to pull them down her legs and toss them aside. Then I place my hands on her knees and say, "Open wide."

She does and I push her thighs up so I can get a clear view and say, "Hold your legs for me."

She grabs her legs and holds as I gently push the lips of her pussy apart. "Uh, well. You're still a virgin."

"How can you tell?" she asks, looking at me through her open legs.

"There's skin there, Aria. He probably wasn't inside you. Either that or he had a very small dick. Because your cherry is good and tight."

"Oh," she says. Frowning. "Well. Shit. I'm still a fucking virgin."

"Do you want me to stop?"

She stares at me for a moment and then shakes her head. "No. It's my birthday." And then she smiles. "It's kind of a good present, right?"

I stare back at her, wondering how the hell I got here.

"Try with your finger first," she says. "Because I don't think your cock is going to fit."

"You have a filthy little mouth," I say.

"Sorry. It's just—"

"It wasn't a criticism," I say. "Just own it."

She smiles and shrugs.

OK, Ryker. You have yourself a virgin. Now what?

It's been a long a time since I had to think about this. But she's right, what we're doing is a gift. Both for her and for me. So I gently place my finger over her clit and begin to massage. "Close your eyes now and enjoy it. If it becomes too much you can tell me to stop and I will. But you have to do this eventually, Aria. And I'll make it feel as good as I can."

"OK," she says, closing her eyes.

I play with her clit for a few seconds, letting the very tip of my finger dip into her pussy just enough to gather up her wetness and make things smoother.

"I like that," she says.

"Yeah," I say. "I'm not inside you yet."

I push the tip in, just a little bit past her hymen, and she gasps. So I stop.

"No, keep going," she says, gritting her teeth. This is why I don't really enjoy being with virgins. It's not going to feel good. It's just an act that needs to be done.

I dip my face down and begin licking her again, deciding to make her come first so she's good and wet when I start putting things inside her.

She goes back to her wiggling and writhing. Her hand dips down to my head without prompting and grips my hair. Guiding me the way I asked her to.

Oh, yeah. She is a very sweet thing.

She begins to hold her breath and then gasps. I watch her through her parted legs, still hiked up so high, her knees are at her shoulders.

"You can come whenever you want," I say. "Just tell me when you're about to so I know."

She bites her lip and nods.

I continue licking, then nipping the soft folds of her pussy carefully. I want to stick all my fingers up inside and make her come on them, but I hold back and be patient.

When I take my thumb to her clit and poke my tongue into her pussy she arches her back and says, "I'm going to come now,"

And as soon as her body goes stiff I shove the whole length of my finger inside her.

"Oh, shit!" she screams. "That hurts!"

"I'm sorry," I say, pumping her. She is good and wet so even though her muscles are tight, practically gripping my finger, it slides in and out easily.

"Does that still feel good?" I ask.

She nods her head and bucks her back again, so I speed up, finger-fucking her like I would a woman with more experience. It takes a few minutes, but holy hell, she comes again, this time gushing all over my finger, and I just...

I just can't believe it.

My dick wants to blow in my jeans. Twice. Unheard of. She is either a very sexual creature or so horny she can't help herself. Either way, I feel like I just won the lottery.

I withdraw my finger and she releases my hair. Then opens her eyes and says, "That's it?"

"What?" I laugh. "You just came twice. That's... very unusual."

"It is?"

"Do you masturbate a lot?"

"Not a lot," she says. "But my sister left me a vibrator so I used that the other night after you left."

I just blink my eyes at her. "I jerked off that night too. Came all over myself thinking about you."

"Are you going to fuck me?"

"Now?" I ask. "Tonight?"

"Please?" she begs. "Just try."

"Uh... I don't think you understand how big my cock is, Aria. My finger," I say, holding it up. "Very, very small compared to my cock."

"Show it to me, so I can see."

Holy shit. I might not be able to fuck her tonight but I'm definitely gonna come all over that sweet face.

I stand up, unbutton and unzip my jeans, then pull them down my hips a little until my cock spills out like a long, thick snake.

85

"Oh," she says.

"Are you disappointed?" I ask.

"No, but you're right. That will never fit inside me."

"Well, it definitely will, Aria. They all fit. It's just not going to feel very good the first time."

She nods, then says, "You don't wear underwear?"

"Not tonight I didn't."

"Because you knew you were gonna see me."

"That's exactly why."

She takes a deep breath, still looking at my cock, and says, "Can I hold it?"

Fuckin' A. This little thing is gonna kill me. "Sure," I say.

She sits up, straightening out her dress skirt, and then reaches for my cock, wrapping her hand around it.

"It's thick. My fingers don't even go all the way around."

I've heard that before. Pretty much every time a girl first holds my cock in her hand. But it always felt contrived. Something they say to be dirty. And that's not at all how it comes out with Aria. It comes out like she just discovered something miraculous. So innocent. She has no idea how hearing her say that makes me feel. No clue at all. She just says it because it's true.

She trains her eyes on mine, her hand pumping along my shaft a little. Like she wants to jerk me off, she's just not sure if she's allowed. "I want to do it."

"Do what?"

"Have sex with you. Real sex. With this inside me."

"I don't know, Aria. I'm gonna hurt you."

"But not on purpose. It's just... something that has to be done. Like you said."

I try to work out a way that doesn't involve her screaming and crying and hating me.

"Please," she begs. "I'm eighteen. I can't end this birthday without feeling like an adult. And this is pretty perfect."

I want to say no. Well, that's a lie. I want to stick my cock inside her right now. But I don't want to hurt her, which means this is going to be a slow, time-consuming process and I'm already ready to blow.

But I take a deep breath and think about how satisfying it will be if I can make her come again. And how I really want to come on her face or her tits, but can't find a way to do that gracefully without putting in some effort.

87

"OK," I say, kicking off my shoes and pulling my pants down so I can kick them away. I take a seat on the couch next her and say, "Climb in my lap."

She swings her leg over, grinning and biting her lip. Her face goes all red with embarrassment when her wet pussy touches the shaft of my cock. And then she straightens out the skirt of her dress so she looks pretty.

I am going to die. She's killing me slowly.

"Do you want to take off your dress?" I ask. "So we can both be naked?"

She thinks about this for a moment, then nods. "Can you help me?"

Can you help me? Dead.

I ease her little pink cardigan down her arms and toss it aside. Then reach around her back and unzip her dress. She lifts her arms and I drag it over her head as her hair spills out and lands over her breasts so perfectly, it feels planned.

She's wearing a pink bra. No cups, just a very thin satin. But her breasts are round, and firm, and her nipples are poking up against the tight fabric.

I squeeze them with both hands and she moans.

"Want my bra off too?" she asks.

"If you want," I say. "It's up to you."

"Do you like fucking girls in their bras?"

Oh, you dirty, little, sweet thing. "Yes," I say. "I kinda do."

"Then I'll leave it on. But now what do I do, Ryker?"

She said my name. God, I don't know why I love that so much, I just do. "Sit up a little," I say. She does. "Now reach down, grab my cock, and point it at your pussy."

She does just that. Then looks at me for what to do next.

"Now, put it up against your pussy and slowly sink down."

She does it too fast and gasps.

"Go slow, I said. Go very slow until you get the head inside, and then just… make yourself sit down, OK?"

"How will I know when the head is inside?"

"You'll know," I say, then reach up to pull her long, burgundy hair away from her face. "But I'll tell you too."

She nods, then begins to slowly try again. I reach between her legs and hold my cock straight and she places both her hands on my shoulders, balancing on her knees before easing down, gasping, and coming up again.

"It's OK," I say. "Just take your time. I'm not in a rush. We've got all night."

She smiles and then a chill runs up her body and comes out as a shudder. Making her bunch her shoulders up and squeeze her tits together.

How did I get this girl in my lap, doing all this with me?

Have no clue.

And this might be her birthday, but this gift is all mine.

"Try again," I say. And to my surprise, I'm patient. I'm totally OK with waiting for her.

She nods her head and presses her lips together. Easing down until she winces and gasps. "Keep going," I say. "Just a little more and my head will be all the way inside you."

She sucks in a deep breath and lets it out, like she's preparing herself for something horrible. Then she sits down a little more, burying her head into my neck as her fingernails claw at my shoulders and back.

"You're doing real well, Aria. I'm inside you now. But there's more of me if you want it. And if you don't, we can stop now."

"No, I want it," she says. Her voice small, and soft, and right up next to my ear.

"OK," I say, petting her hair. "OK. Then just… force yourself to sit. And no matter what, don't stop. If you just do it real fast it'll be over. The pain will go away, I promise. And then you'll know what it feels like to have a man fully inside you. I'll make you feel good, I promise."

She swallows so hard I can hear it. Almost a gulp. She begins shaking a little, like she's cold, or maybe nervous. So I wrap my arms around her and hold her close to me, trying to make her warm and feel secure.

"Count to three," she says.

Oh, I'm so dead.

"One," I say. "Two. Three."

And on three she does three things.

She sinks down hard on to my cock.

She screams and tenses up, arching her back and struggling in my tight grip around her body.

And she goes still and looks at me.

I kiss her. I kiss this silly, sweet little thing like I've never kissed anyone in my life. And then I whisper, "Are you OK?"

She nods, and whispers back, strain and pain in her voice, "But don't move. Please don't move."

"I won't," I say, taking my kisses to her neck. "You get to do all the moving. When you're ready, lift up just a little bit and then sink down again."

"Oh, God."

"No, no," I say, petting her hair. "Shhh. The more you move, the better it feels, and the easier it gets. Trust me, I'm going to make you come again. And when we're finished that's the only thing you'll remember."

"OK," she says. Lifting her hips up.

I grab her ass and say, "Not too far. You want to keep me inside you."

She eases back down again, hissing air.

"That's good," I say. "Just keep doing that over and over again."

She lifts up again and I can feel how wet she is. So fucking wet. Virgin wet. And then I realize that's probably blood.

But I don't say anything thing about the blood because I don't want to freak her out.

"You're doing good," I say, surprised once again at how patient I am.

Pretty soon she's moving a little faster. Not taking her time. Not hissing in pain.

"I told you," I said. "I told you it would feel good. Now listen carefully. And look at me."

She stops moving and picks her head up off my shoulder so her eyes can find mine. She looks sleepy but she's not sleepy. That is the look of lust, she just doesn't realize it yet.

"I'm going to make you come, but in order to do that, I have to touch your pussy as I fuck you. Not you fuck me, like you've been doing. But *me* fuck *you*. Do you understand?"

She shakes her head no.

"I'm going to move now. Not you. I'll be in charge now, not you. That's how it has to be if you want to end this with another orgasm. OK?"

She nods, pouting.

"Don't worry," I whisper. "You'll like it."

I reach around her and unclasp her bra. She shoots me a questioning look, but I just mouth the words, *trust me*.

She rolls her eyes with teenage attitude and I take that as a yes.

She helps me get her bra down her arms and then a sudden wave of embarrassment overtakes her and she covers her breasts with her arms.

I pull them away, shaking my head. "No. Don't cover yourself up, Aria. I want to watch your tits bounce when I start fucking you."

She looks very nervous. But we've come this far, we're not quitting now.

I ease my hips down to the edge of the couch so I can flatten my hand along her belly and caress her clit with my fingers. I hold on to her hip with my other hand and begin thrusting my hips upward.

"Oh, shit!" she gasps.

"Just relax," I say, rubbing her clit faster.

This makes her close her eyes and the next time I thrust upward, I bounce her on my legs so her tits bounce with her.

"Ahhhh," she gasps again. Her mouth is open wide in surprise.

Yes. That's what I want to see as I fuck the sweet virginity out of this girl. I thrust again, and again, and again and each time her tits bounce higher and her mouth says, "Oh! Oh! Oh!"

All the while my fingers are playing with her clit like crazy and my cock has decided enough is enough, the time to be patient is over and now it's time to *really* fuck. So I thrust harder and harder, and then I bend her over and hold her to my chest as I reach around and play with her ass and then—

She screams.

Not the scream of a virgin trying to stuff a fat cock head into her pussy, but the scream of a girl who has now come three times in one night.

And I'm ready too. The agony of this night has caught up with me and I can't hold it in anymore. My time has come.

Literally.

Because I pull her off me, shove her down to the floor so she's on her knees, and then I sit up and shoot my load all over her tits.

She looks at me in... I'm not sure. Horror? Surprise? Disgust? Possibly all three. But I didn't wear a condom—probably should've, but fuck it—and so I couldn't come inside her.

It has to go somewhere.

"Holy shit!" she says, scooting away from me. "You just—"

"Came on your tits and it was hot as fuck," I say, sinking back down to the couch. "By the way, you're on the pill?"

95

"No," she says. And then she screws up her face and says, "Oh, my God, we didn't use a condom. I'm gonna get a disease!"

"Relax, sweet thing," I say. "I'm clean, I promise. I'll get a clean bill of health for you, if you need it. And that's why I came on your tits. I know what I'm doing. Not my first rodeo."

"Ewwww," she says, crinkling up her nose. "I think I will need that clean bill of health."

I smile at her and beckon her with a finger. "Come here."

"No," she says, uncertain. "I don't think so. You should leave now."

"What?" I ask.

"No, I mean… well. Yes. You should leave. It was great and all. Like seriously, it was. And thank you. I learned a lot tonight and no more pesky—" That's when she sees the blood on my cock. "Eww. Oh, God. Oh, man. Just… like I said," she says, covering her eyes so she doesn't have to look at my dick. "Thank you. I will remember it always. It's probably one of the best deflowerings ever in the history of the world and…" She smiles and peeks at me from behind her fingers. "Yeah." Raising her eyebrows. "Pret-*ty* good! But no, you gotta get out now. I have class in the morning and whew, I'm tired and I actually have a headache. So…" She smiles at me. "Goodbye. I need a shower." She gets up and starts walking away, teasing me with her tight, perky ass. But then turns and says, "Oh. And you can just slip that clean bill of health under the door of my cube, OK? Thanks!"

I just sit there for a few minutes, listening to her hum in the shower like she just had the best fuck of her life—which it was, and it's not because it was her first, either—and wonder what the fuck just happened.

Did she just… one-night-stand me?

CHAPTER NINE

I wake up the next morning thinking about Ryker. But not because I'm having visions of wedding bells or anything, it's because I'm sore as fuck. I'm talking… it feels like his giant cock is stuck up inside me. So weird, and kinda good too, but also sore as fuck.

When I came out of the shower I was totally nervous that he didn't get my hint and was still here, but I found a note by my phone that said, *I got your number now. I'll call you.* So whew, he was gone. But then, *Oh, shit. He's gonna call me.*

I don't want to see him again. He's too old for me. And, well, hot, yes. And very good at the fucking stuff. But no. Too old. My dad would freak out if he knew and he probably already thinks something is up after the way Ryker boxed me in in front of the window last night at the co-op.

So no. That's the end of the hot land developer-slash-drummer who's very good at deflowering virgins.

The. End.

Period.

Story over.

But then, while I'm lying in bed, my phone rings on my nightstand and who is it?

Him. He even put his contact in my phone so it says Ryker North.

The guy who said this is a one-time thing and then made me come three times.

What is his deal?

I consider ignoring it but I'm out of my league. He has a job, and a car, and money, and he's a full-fledged grown-up, so I know the only way to get rid of this guy is to tell it to him straight.

"Hello?" I say, after tabbing the answer button.

"Aria," he says. "I made a doctor's appointment today to ease your mind about sex diseases."

"Oh, good!" I say. "Perfect. When you get those test results—"

"Yeah, slip it under your cube door."

"Exactly."

"So what are you doing today?"

"What?"

"Plans? What are your plans?"

"Um… I start my class today."

"What time is that?"

"Eleven." Why am I even telling him this? He's no one.

"What time is it over?"

"Two," I say. "Why?"

"I'll pick you up."

"No," I say. "Nope. My dad is picking me up."

"Then I guess we'll both pick you up. I'll be out front of the main entrance of the college at two. You should be there."

The call drops and I just stare at the phone. "What the fuck?" Is he some kind of stalker? Did he change his mind about the one-night thing? I thought we were using each other?

What do I do? Do I meet him there or blow him off?

I can't think about this right now. The first real day of my pretend new life starts now. And I'm not a virgin. I had deflowering sex with a totally hot older man.

Which is very cool and will make a great story for when I go back to high school in two weeks, but right now, he's sorta cramping my style.

I'm gonna meet a hot kid my own age—or sorta close to it—and date him for two weeks. And then I'm gonna go back to school and brag about my adventures and one of the hot guys who really are my own age will fall into lust with me and then I'll go to prom with him.

Oh, my God. I could be prom queen!

Or maybe none of that will happen, but it could! It totally could as long as Ryker North isn't hanging around.

My phone dings a text in my hand so I look down at the screen.

Ryker: *Don't wear underwear today. I want to play with your pussy in the car.*

What?

My fingers start flying in reply. *Sicko. I'm not getting in your car.*

My phone rings again. Guess who?

"What?" I say.

"You really don't want to see me again?"

"You said one night! I don't understand."

102

"Yeah, but… you're like eighteen years old."

"So?"

"You're young and you have romantic delusions and think I'm your boyfriend now, right?"

I laugh. "What?"

"I'm kidding," he says. "Just fucking with you. Sort of. I want to see you again."

"I don't think it's a good idea."

"Why not?"

"How old are you?"

"Thirty-five."

"That's why."

"I'm a pretty hot thirty-five."

"You really are." I giggle. "But no. I can't. I'm sorry. My dad would hate it. And I'm into guys my own age."

"What guys?"

"No one in particular, dummy. Just… guys."

"So be into me until you find one."

I pause, thinking about this.

"OK? We good?"

"Ryker—"

"I really am going to get you off in the car, so that text was not a request."

"You can't tell me not to wear underwear. Besides, you said the underwear sex was hot."

"It is. But knowing you're sitting next to me in a dress without panties because you want my fingers inside you as we drive is hot too."

Holy shit. This guy does not fuck around.

"I'll tell you what. You can wear them to school but take them off before you get in the car."

"I'm not getting in your car!"

"You are, Aria. So just do what I say. You'll like it, I promise."

Then he drops me! Fucker hangs up on me!

So I call him back but he sends me straight to voicemail!

And oh, boy, do I leave a voicemail. "You know what?" I tell the phone. "You're kind of a pervert. Taking advantage of me and my flower. Being all patient and hot and telling me to fuck you as slow as I want." I pause. "Jesus. When I say it like that—never mind. I'm not getting in your car. I'm not even wearing a dress today! So ha!"

Then I drop him.

And get up. Unable to stop thinking about him because his ghost cock is still up inside me.

God, why does it feel like this? Am I damaged?

I wish I had a friend from school who knows what it's like to have hot monster-cock sex. If April were here I could ask her. But she's so busy and there's like twenty hours of time difference between us, so I can't. Besides, she'd probably tell my mom and then I'd get a safe sex lecture because—well, I totally need that lecture.

I pick up my phone and call him again. Once more getting voicemail. "And," I say, picking up where I left off. "And you didn't even use a condom! Not your first rodeo, huh? Asshole!"

I drop him and go back to fuming confusion.

A few minutes later my phone rings again, and yup. It's Ryker. "What?"

"I apologize," he says.

"For which part?"

"The condom," he says. "That's the only mistake I made."

105

"Hmmm," I say, trying to think up another mistake. "You did kiss me when I was still seventeen."

"You did lie to me."

"Yeah, but you already knew."

"Touché. I'm sorry."

Hmmm. Told him.

"So..." he says.

"So..." I say.

"Wear a dress and take off your panties before you get in my car."

"What kind of car do you have?"

I swear to God, I can hear him smile on the other end of the phone. "Dodge Challenger."

"Hmm," I say. "That kinda says sexy drummer."

"Yeah, it kinda does."

"Old or new?"

"New. I'm trying to be eco-friendly." Which just makes me snort. "Hey, it's a helluva lot better than the old ones."

"Still a gas guzzler."

"Sorry, I'm never getting a Prius."

"You could get a Tesla."

He laughs. "I guess I could."

"So... if you show up in a Tesla, I'll wear a dress, take off my panties, and get in your car."

I drop him. And smile.

Take that, you sexy, hot, tattooed drummer with amazing deflowering skills.

My phone dings a text. It says one word.

Done.

So... it turns out that guys who take Photoshop certification classes during spring break are all old geeks. I'm the only girl in the whole class, which is so disappointing, but also makes me the center of attention. Especially since I'm wearing one of April's dresses. It's tame, for her. But for me it's kinda flashy.

She wore it to church last Easter and never put it on again. But her idea of a church dress is unique. So it's a short peach dress with a flirty chiffon skirt, with a bazillion pearls on the sewn-on belt. The front has a scoop neck and there's pretty cap sleeves, but the back is too low to wear a bra, so...

107

I wear the panties to school, but not the bra.

I'm pretty sure every single old geek can tell, too.

And it's just a little bit windy standing out in front of the main entrance, so when Ryker pulls up—wearing dark sunglasses, a white button-down shirt with his sleeves rolled up to reveal his tattoos, and a pair of gray slacks, all inside a smokin' hot freaking Tesla!—I feel a little bit like Marilyn Monroe standing over that gust of air coming up from a street vent. Except in peach.

The engine roars as he idles. Waiting for me to walk over to the car.

I open the door, slide in and gape at this beautiful monster. Both of them. Him and the car.

"Nice, right?" he says. "It's next year's prototype. And full disclosure, it's not mine. I had to cash in a major favor to pick you up in this."

I try to hide my smile but I can't. Not even behind my hand, because I'm giggling.

"That's funny, huh?"

"Well," I say, straightening my skirt, then flipping it up to flash him a quick look. "Your reward awaits."

"You're ridiculous," he says, pulling away from the curb. "All the rewards belong to you, Aria. You hungry?"

"I can't go into a restaurant without panties."

"How else am I going to play with your pussy in public?"

"What?"

"You heard me. I'm quite annoyed at being dismissed last night after I took such good care of you."

"Did you go to the doctor?" I ask.

He side-eyes me. "Yes. Results in a few days. But I'm clean. I promise. Besides," he says, lifting up the center console. "I brought these."

I peek inside and laugh again. Condoms. "You're the one who said one-night stand, Ryker."

"Yeah, but we bonded, right? I deflowered you." Then he looks over at me and smiles. Winking behind his glasses. I can tell because his cheek lifts up a little.

"You wanted to stay over?" I ask.

"Maybe. But forget it now. I got your rules down. Fuck you hard and leave you immediately."

I sit back in my seat and smile, enjoying the sunshine on my face as we drive around. "So where are you going to do these nasty things to me?"

"The Corinthian Hotel."

"Stop it. We're not playing these games there."

"Why not?"

"It's classy."

"You in that dress with no underwear is classy."

"So classy." I giggle again. And it's weird. Because I don't know him. Like at all. But I feel like I do. I feel like we're known each other forever and this is just one of hundreds of times we've been out together.

But we do go to the hotel. He pulls up in the valet and then someone's opening my door, and I have to be very careful not to flash anyone because seriously, this skirt is too flirty to not wear underwear. But then Ryker is there, looking like a hot drummer, and he takes my hand and leads me inside to the restaurant.

They serve tea in the lobby seating area, and I've had tea here with my parents quite a few times, but I've never been to the restaurant.

"North," he tells the maître d', holding up two fingers.

Those two fingers were inside me last night.

"This way, Mr. North," the maître d' says.

We follow him into a dark corner half-circle booth with low lighting and I scoot in, all the way into the far corner, and Ryker scoots in right beside me, putting his arm around my shoulder.

Well, I will say one thing. None of the boys in high school could ever pull this date off, that's for sure.

Ryker takes his sunglasses off and sets them on the table, then turns towards me a little and says, "Meet any cute boys at school?"

"No," I say.

"Mmmm-hmm," he says, picking up his menu. "Called that one."

"You didn't call anything," I say, picking up my menu.

But he grabs it from me and says, "I'm ordering for you."

"You don't even know me."

"I guess I'll learn fast then." And he winks again.

He's being kind of... dickish. I guess that's a word. Letting me know he's slightly annoyed with me. But at the same time he's doing everything right. The car, the clothes, the restaurant, the booth. All of it makes me feel wonderfully taken care of.

"Thank you," I say.

"For what?"

"For all of it. It was... nice."

"Nice?" He cocks an eyebrow at me.

111

"Nice as in thoughtful," I say. "All of it. You didn't need to be so careful with me, so I just want you to know that I appreciate that."

"God, Aria," he says, rubbing his jaw with his hand.

"What?"

"You're so fucking *sweet*."

"Thanks?" I say. "I guess."

"No, really," he says, taking my hand and kissing it. "You're fucking killing me. You are honest, and willing." He waggles his eyebrows at me. "But most of all... just sweet. I can't stop thinking about it. You're just a nice girl. A really nice girl."

"Aww," I say, bumping my shoulder into his chest. "Thank you."

"I want to keep seeing you. What do I have to do to make that happen?"

I crinkle my nose at him. "You mean... be my boyfriend?"

"Maybe." He shrugs. "But it doesn't have to be that, I guess."

"Hmm," I say, thinking about this. "I mean, I like you. I do. And if you keep pursuing me I will give in and I will see you again. But you can't come to prom with me."

He laughs a little too loud, then shakes his head and looks down at his menu again. "We can start there and see what happens."

When the waiter comes he orders us both water with lime and then puts his hand on my leg and slides it under my skirt.

"Not now," I say, trying to swat him away.

But he just grips my leg tight—tight enough to tickle and make me gasp—then says, "Yes. Now. While we order. I want to see how you handle it."

"How I handle it?"

"Coming in public."

"Ryker," I whisper. "No."

"Oh, yeah. I lived up to my end of the deal, now you have to live up to yours. I want you to feel out of control. And ultimately you are in control. Aria. You can get up and walk out any time you want. I'll take you home. Leave you alone. But I like to play games and this is the one I want to play with you. So you're not in control. I am."

"Jesus," I mumble.

"Should we go? Or stay?" He slides his fingers right between my legs as he says that and even though I'm still super sore and it totally feels like there's still a cock inside me, I'm also wet and hot for him.

"Stay," I say.

And then he leans over and kisses me on the mouth. "You're not going to regret it. Also, you should know. You're mine now. So no one, and I do mean no one, but us will know what's happening under your skirt. Got it?"

"OK," I say, hesitantly.

"That means you can't scream out, or moan, or whine, or squeak, or make any of those noises you were making last night. Understand?"

I take in a deep breath and nod. "OK."

"Good," he whispers, leaning over to kiss my mouth. "I'm going to get you off right now, before we order."

"Right now?"

"Right now. So concentrate."

But it's very hard to concentrate when there's several dozen business people in here with us and wait staff is bustling past our table every few seconds.

"Open your legs a little more," he whispers, angling his body towards mine.

I do, and the tip of his finger begins playing with my clit as he gazes down into my eyes and says, "Now talk to me. Tell me about your day so no one knows what I'm doing."

"My day was spent thinking about you."

"Yeah? What kind of thoughts did you have?"

His finger slips down my slit and begins to push into my entrance.

"I thought about... how I could still feel you inside me when I woke up. And how sore I was."

"Does this hurt?" he says, pushing his finger up a little further.

"Two waters with lime," the waiter says, placing our drinks on the table. "Do you need a few more minutes?" he asks me.

And in that exact same moment, Ryker's finger begins flicking my clit.

"Yes, please," I say, barely managing not to squeak.

"Very well," the waiter says with a small bow. "Take your time."

"I don't think we'll need much time," Ryker says. "Give us two minutes."

"Two minutes," the waiter says. "Be right back."

"Two minutes?" I say.

"Two minutes, sweet thing. And keep talking."

115

"Keep talking," I repeat, just as he sticks his finger back inside me.

"You can lean back a little, if you need to. But not too much. And don't make faces."

"I'm not making faces."

"You are making faces." He laughs. "You look like someone is fingering you under the tablecloth right now."

"Oh, God."

"Minute and a half."

"Put it all the way in," I say. "And fuck me with it. Quick."

"Holy shit, Aria," he says. But he does what I ask. He slides his finger all the way up inside me until it's so clear he is fingering me under the table—I feel like everyone is watching.

They aren't. Or maybe they're pretending not to. But it turns me on to think that they are. And one more flick of Ryker's thumb on my clit and I do it. I come. Not a big climax, but a slow, gushing wet one that makes him lean in and kiss me right on the mouth.

"Are you ready to order?" the waiter says. Just a few seconds after I remove my finger from Aria's pussy and hold it under the table. I want her to lick it. She will lick it.

"Yes. Miss Amherst will have the truffle grilled cheese and I'll have the ribeye sandwich."

"Very good choices." The waiter smiles and takes the menus. Then he looks at Aria and says, "I'm sure you'll love the grilled cheese, honey," before walking off.

"What was that?" Aria says.

"What was what?" I ask, leaning in to her neck to kiss her. "I want to take you in the bathroom an—"

"Grilled cheese?" she says.

"What's wrong with grilled cheese?" I ask, pulling away from her.

117

"Am I five?"

"It's *truffle* grilled cheese, Aria. For grown-ups."

She just makes a face.

"OK, so you don't like grilled cheese. Noted."

"I like grilled cheese, it's just"—she makes a noise of frustration—"I feel five!"

"Aria," I say, leaning back in to her neck. "I'm playing with your pussy in public. There is no reason to feel like you're five."

"Yeah," she says, pushing my hand away from her leg. "Stop that. Everyone is looking over here."

"No one's looking," I say, glancing around. No one is. Everyone is having lunch.

"I feel like… a toy. Like some plaything. And you know what? I'm not."

"Uh… OK," I say, calmly leaning back against the booth. "I thought we *were* playing around, so that could be the reason."

"Don't do that."

"Do what? Why are you so upset with me? I'm sorry about the grilled cheese. I didn't choose it because it's called grilled cheese. I chose it because truffles are delicious and fancy."

She makes a face and takes a deep breath. "I don't think I want to be here."

"Here?" I say, pointing down at the table. "Or with me?"

She looks away.

"OK," I say, flagging the waiter as he rushes by. "Excuse me? Can we cancel our order? Our plans have changed."

"Certainly, sir. And no charge for the water."

"Thanks," I say, getting out my wallet to leave a tip.

"We don't have to leave."

"Clearly we do, Aria." I scoot out of the booth on one side and she scoots out on the other. We don't hold hands as we walk back through the restaurant. She leads the way, chin up, stiff posture, hands holding her skirt close to her legs, and I follow, wondering why I bother with the young ones.

There is a reason people tend to date others their own age, right? Compatibility and stuff like that?

"Where should I drop you?" I ask her, once the valet delivers the car.

"Just... home."

"Fine," I say, pulling away from the hotel.

119

There's quite a bit of traffic so this makes the awkward silence even more awkward. Finally, I can't take it anymore. "Aria," I say. "What's the real problem? Is it my choice of food or the fact that you felt uncomfortable with what we were doing or—"

"You know what it is?" she says, looking straight ahead.

"That's what I'm asking."

"It's wrong."

"What's wrong? My hands on your body in public? Because that's kind of the point, right? We were just playing around. Having some secret fun. It's supposed to feel wrong, and daring, and exciting, and—"

"That's not how it felt," she says.

"Well, it was until I ordered you truffle grilled cheese."

She huffs.

"You were laughing, having a good time, and then—bam. You were pissed. So what's wrong?"

"Why are you even here with me? This was supposed to be a one-night thing."

"Right. We talked about this already. I changed my mind and you changed yours. And clearly, you've changed it again. So fine. You don't want me around,

I'll drop you off and never talk to you again. That work for you, princess?"

She doesn't say anything else the rest of the ride back to her sister's apartment. When I pull up to the front of the house, she gets out without a word, closes the door, and walks away.

I sit there for a second. Watch her go through the door, and then shake my head and drive away.

This is why I don't date eighteen-year-old girls.

But back at the office I can't get her out of my mind. I messed up. I did something. Not the grilled cheese, that's just what triggered her new feelings. I made a mistake somewhere. Misjudged her.

And even though I want to pretend that it's all cool, just another one-night stand... I can't.

I took her virginity last night.

And I liked it.

I might even like her.

"What's up your ass today?" Ozzy says, coming into my office and flopping down on a chair. "We're totally on track to purchase three more houses and one more building in the Gingerbread. And the festival is coming

121

along nicely. July fourth is gonna be a blast. We'll probably have sold several houses by then. Two are going on the market—" Then he stops. "Are you even listening to me?"

I stare at him for a second. "You ever date a younger woman?"

He laughs. "All the time."

"How young?" I ask.

He shrugs. "The girl I went out with last weekend was twenty-seven. Seeing her again tonight, in fact."

"No, I mean *young*," I say. "As in really young."

"How young?" he asks, with a totally different tone.

"Eighteen," I say.

"Oh, dude. No. No, no, no. Don't go there. That's a child. And yeah, they look good, but there's nothing there, Ryker. It's just fluff."

"Yeah." I sigh, leaning back in my chair. "You're probably right."

"I am right. I tried to date a girl who was twenty once and it was fun for like… two days. Then she just went all stupid on me."

"Stupid how?" I ask.

"You know… 'You're too old,'" he says, mimicking a girl's voice. "'I can't be seen with you in public. People will talk or think I'm your daughter.'"

"Hmmm. How old were you?"

"Shit, I was only thirty at the time." He shakes his head at me. "Thirty-five and eighteen, Ryk? It's never gonna work. Just get rid of her. Let her down easy, but yeah. Get rid of her."

I nod. "Sure. Yeah. I'll do that." But I don't have to do that because she already got rid of me.

"OK, well, I just came in here to tell you I'm having a meeting with the bankers Friday afternoon to put together the next loan package for the current resident rehabs."

"Cool," I say, barely caring. Why is this girl on my mind? Why do I care?

"Cool," Ozzy says. "You're coming though, right? To the meeting? Because this is a new bank and they've already raised questions about how much we've borrowed for this project. I know we're extended, but we're not overextended. We can manage one more loan. Besides, we can't get the neighborhood on our side unless we show them we're on their side. We need this loan package."

"Sure," I say. "I'll definitely be there."

"So what are you doing tonight? You wanna come have drinks with Sheila and me?"

"Who's Sheila again?"

"The one I met on Wednesday," he says getting to his feet.

"Right. No, I think I'm gonna go play some skins tonight, actually."

"Creative Co-op," he says, shooting me with his finger. "Such a good move. They're gonna love us. There's not gonna be any bad press with this gentrification."

I don't say anything, just stare at him.

"Gotcha," he says. "You're in a dick mood so that's my cue to leave. Catch you tomorrow, Ryker."

I wave at him as he leaves. Watching him through the open door of my office as he talks to the staff and gathers his stuff.

Nothing up there but fluff, he said.

It's probably true, too. Hell, Aria even told me she's looking to date someone her own age. And she's thinking about college and prom.

I should just forget about her. Pretend it never happened.

But that night, when I go in to the Creative Co-Op, I can't pretend I'm not disappointed that she's not there. Because I'm totally pretending to be working on something so she can get a glimpse of me. Or whatever...

I play the drums well into the early morning hours and tell myself I won't drive by her place to see if the light's on. But I do. And it's not.

I go into the co-op every night after too. Hoping she'll be there. But the only person I see is the ballerina, who might have a thing for me because she hangs out and talks to me in her leotard and tutu and flirts, and giggles, even when I make it very clear I'm not interested.

I drive by Aria's house on my way home each night and by Friday I'm driving by in the mornings and taking a late lunch so I can catch her coming out of class at the college.

Not once do I even get a glimpse of her.

But that afternoon I have a reason to call her.

My test results came in. Clean, just like I promised. And I don't want to slide them under her cube door.

Because I really don't think she's even been in to the co-op since she walked away on Monday.

She doesn't pick up my call. Sends me straight to voicemail. I sigh as the beep sounds. "Hey, Aria. Hope you're well. Just wanted to let you know my tests came back clean. So no worries, OK? And I'll be at the co-op tonight. My regular time. So if you want to see them…" God. I feel so stupid right now. "You know what to do."

I end the call and slide my phone across the desk, glancing up at the clock.

It's fucking Friday afternoon and I have no date. Last Friday I met her. One week. I've known this girl one week.

And she's the only thing I can think about.

"Ready?" Ozzy says. "The car is waiting."

"For?" I ask.

"Jesus Christ," Ozzy says. "What the hell is your problem this week? Drinks with the banker? Ringing any bells?"

"Ah, yeah. Right. That. Yeah, I'm ready. Let's go."

CHAPTER ELEVEN

"Who was that?" my father asks, after I send the incoming call to voicemail. I've been spending all my time with him this week. Letting him pick me up from class to take me out to dinner, then dropping me off at home after. Trying to forget about Ryker North and his hot fingers between my legs.

"No one," I say.

"No one?" my father asks. We're sitting in the Corinthian Hotel this afternoon. He's meeting clients after our early dinner, so we just came here. "Didn't look like no one. Did you meet a nice boy at school?" He smiles at me.

"Ugggh, Dad. I'm not talking about boys with you!"

"So there is a boy?" he says.

"No!" I say. "There's no boy, I swear."

It's not even a lie because Ryker North is a man. He hasn't been a boy for a very long time.

"Well, when there is, I need to meet him."

"You will," I say. "Don't worry, Dad. I would never date anyone you didn't approve of first."

"Did you enjoy your meal?" he asks a little while later. "I've never heard of truffle grilled cheese. Interesting. But you usually like the club."

Yup. I went there. Because I felt like a total ass after that whole meltdown I had with Ryker over this sandwich and you know what? He was right. It's not for kids. I don't even like it. "It's OK," I say, then wrinkle my nose. "Should've gotten the club."

"We have time. Would you like to order something else?"

"Umm... yeah," I say. "I would. April didn't exactly stock the fridge before she left and I haven't had a chance to go shopping."

My father flags down a waiter and orders me a club, then looks at his watch. "I'm going to go check the lobby, sweetheart. See if the clients are here yet. Be right back."

"Sure, Dad," I say.

He walks off and I take a moment to check my voicemail.

"Hey, Aria. Hope you're well. Just wanted to let you know my tests came back clean. So no worries, OK? And I'll be at the co-op tonight. My regular time. So if you want to see them... you know what to do."

I know what to do.

Actually, I don't know what to do. I have no clue what to do. I thought it would be pretty easy to forget about Ryker North. He's way too old for me. And he's bossy. And that whole thing in the restaurant—this restaurant—it was weird. Hot and all that. But weird. I can't seem to make up my mind. Did I like it? Did I hate it? Was it embarrassing? Was it fun?

It was all those things and that's so confusing.

He's confusing. Hell, I'm confusing.

But I'd be lying if I said I wasn't still interested in him. I know he's been at the co-op because I've walked by there every night and I could hear him playing. I want to go inside and say something. Apologize for overreacting.

But did I overreact?

I'm not sure.

But he'll be there tonight and he gave me a reason to stop by, right? Which maybe means he wants to see me too.

Should I go over there? Or should I ignore this message? He said his test results came back clean and I believe him. I wasn't really that worried about sex diseases anyway. He's a grown-up. He knows how to avoid that kind of situation. I'd be more worried about a boy my own age because they're stupid, and impulsive, and safe sex isn't exactly the most pressing matter when the mood hits.

"Aria," my father says, suddenly at the table again. "I'd like you to meet my clients, Oswald Herrington III"—he pans his hand to one man—"and Ryker North. They're developers who..."

But I don't hear the rest. Because Ryker North is standing next to my dad—in the same restaurant where he fingered me last week—and my dad is patting him on the back and smiling like they are old friends.

Oh, my God. *Are* they old friends?

I just sit there, my mouth open, and stare at them like an idiot as they all unbutton their suit coats and settle into their chairs.

"Um..." I say. "I was just leaving." And as soon as I say that the waiter comes, deposits my club sandwich in front of me, and removes the mostly uneaten truffle grilled cheese.

"There you go, sweetie," he says. "And no charge for this one," indicating the plate in his hand.

"Oh, Aria," my father says. "I forgot you ordered another plate."

"She can stay," the Oswald guy says. "Go ahead," he says, looking at me. "Finish your meal. But I have to warn you, we're pretty boring."

He smiles at me, then my father, and my father must like this idea, because he smiles back and says, "Sure, Aria. Finish your dinner."

Finish my dinner. God, if I didn't feel like a child last week, I definitely do now.

I look down at my plate and start nibbling the end of a French fry.

I glance up at Ryker and find him staring at me as my father starts talking about business. But he puts up a hand, smiles, and says, "I'm sorry. Was that the world-famous truffle grilled cheese you just sent back?"

"Oh, she thought it would be like a regular grilled cheese," my father says. "But she didn't care for it."

"Oh," Ryker says. "I'm sorry to hear that. It's one of my favorites here. I get it all the time. In fact," he says, looking at Oswald, "I'm gonna order it tonight."

"Maybe I should just take it home—"

"No, no, no," Ryker says. "Stay. Don't let us interrupt your dinner."

131

"No," I say, motioning to our waiter. "Excuse me, can I get a take-home bag for this, please?"

"Sure," he says, smiling as he grabs my plate and bustles off to pack it up.

"Are you sure, Aria?" my dad says. "We don't mind you hanging around."

"No, I'm fine, Dad. I'm sure you have a lot of boring grown-up things to discuss. I'll just be the fourth wheel." I pull out my phone and start tapping. "I'll just order a car home."

"We can take you home," Oswald says, pulling out his phone too. "Our company driver just left. He's probably only a block or two away." He smiles at my dad, who smiles back like this is the perfect solution. His precious daughter being treated preciously by his clients.

I want to gag. And open my mouth to protest but Oswald is already talking to the driver. He ends the call and says, "He's still out front. Ryker, show Miss Amherst where the car is while I go over some things with Mr. Amherst, will you?"

Ryker says, "Sure."

Just as I say, "That's not necessary."

And my dad says, "Thank you, Mr. North."

And the waiter plops my takeaway bag down in front of me and says, "There you go, sweetie, all set now."

I just sit there for a moment, unsure what to do, just very, *very* sure that I should not be alone with Ryker North while my father is in the same room.

But Ryker stands, buttoning his suit coat, and says, "Right this way, Miss Amherst," as he comes over to pull out my chair.

This little display of chivalry makes my father absolutely *beam*.

I get up, walk over to my dad, kiss him on the cheek, and say, "Thank you, Daddy. See you on Monday."

"Have a nice weekend, sweetheart!" he calls. But then he waggles his finger at me and says, "Just don't have too much fun!"

And Ryker North pans his hand towards the front of the restaurant and says, "This way."

I walk in front of him and he makes no move to catch up to me or talk until we enter the main lobby of the hotel, at which point he says, "So the truffle grilled cheese was a bad decision all the way around, huh?"

"I don't think we should talk."

"I'm sorry," he says, ignoring my statement. "I shouldn't have… well, any of it. So I'm sorry."

133

"Hmm," I say, as we near the lobby doors.

"What's that mean?"

"Any of it?" I ask.

"Look, Aria," he says, waving me forward into the revolving door. He steps in with me and in those two seconds of absolute privacy he says, "I like you. But you deserve better."

And then we're outside walking towards a black car, and a driver is pulling the rear door open for me, and I don't even get a moment to say anything, because I just scoot inside and the door closes behind me.

I look over at Ryker, trying to get one last look, but he's already turned back to his business meeting.

I take deep, deep breaths on my way back to the table. Ozzy cannot know how close we came to blowing up this deal. We need this. Our whole plan depends on this one last loan to get us through the project so it actually pays off.

But Aria. Jesus. Why is the universe fucking with me? It's bad enough that I can't get that girl off my mind, even worse that I took her virginity and then fingered her in this very restaurant, and now I find out her father holds our future in his hands.

"There he is!" Ozzy says. "Did you make sure Mr. Amherst's daughter got in the car safely?"

I smile at her father. "She's well taken care of, sir. No issues, I promise."

He beams at me, then looks at Ozzy. "Well, I'm very impressed with your thoughtful plan for the Gingerbread neighborhood, Mr. Herrington. As I'm sure you're aware, this neighborhood is dear to my heart. My older daughter lives there and we started the Creative Co-Op to support the local artists."

"We know," Ozzy says. "Ryker here is a drummer from way back. We actually just purchased a space over there this week. Ryker's getting back to his bad-boy roots!"

"No," I say. "No bad-boy roots."

"Ah, come on," Ozzy says. "He's being modest. This guy grew up with Kenner McConnell. They taught each other drums back in high school."

"Who?" Mr. Amherst asks.

"Nobody," I say.

"Nobody?" Ozzy says, laughing. "He's only the drummer of one of the greatest rock bands of all time."

"Who?" Amherst asks again.

"It's not important," I say. And I'm kinda irritated with Ozzy for mentioning it. It was a weird time in my life, and not a good weird, either. And Ozzy never approved of that old life, so right now he's only doing this to impress Aria's father. Even worse, I'm not sure it's working.

"Son of a Jack," Ozzy says, doubling down and ignoring my cues that I really don't want Aria's dad's first impression of me to be one associated with the most controversial bands to hit the scene in the last two decades.

"Oh," Amherst says. "I think I've heard of them. I'm pretty sure April, my older daughter, saw them in concert a few times." Then he winks at me. "She's my outrageous one. She's in Australia photographing models right now or I'd introduce you. But Aria..." He sighs. "Aria is my sweet one. She's not into that kind of scene."

Jesus Christ. I'm going to hell for what I did with his sweet thing of a daughter. What was I thinking?

"In fact," Ozzy says, "aren't they on tour right now? I think they're coming here to play over Fourth of July." He looks excitedly at Amherst. "Ryker will get in touch with them and see if they have time to meet your daughter."

"Oh, I'm sure she would love that!" Amherst beams.

I just give up and nod. "Sure. Sure. I'll see what I can do."

The rest of the meeting goes pretty much like that. Ozzy and Amherst hitting it off wildly and me picturing what my eternal sentence in hell might look like. Because it's very clear that the whole reason Amherst gave his younger daughter a big old diamond ring for her eighteenth birthday was because it's a giant hands-off signal for anyone who thinks they can take his place in her sweet, young heart.

137

But... success. Amherst, Ozzy, and I leave the restaurant with a firm handshake deal on the final loan we'll need to finish the project.

I beg off after that, telling Ozzy that I'm just gonna walk home and I'll see him on Monday, while he takes the car back to the office to go over the loan papers.

When I get home I change into jeans and a t-shirt and wait for nine o'clock to roll around so I can go over to the co-op and drum off some steam. I hadn't realized how much I've missed music until this past week and used it to take my mind off Aria.

Didn't work. In fact, it made me think of her more. The way she came in that night of her birthday. Her father outside in the car while I went all alpha on her.

The devil is saving me a special place in hell for all this, I can feel it. How is it that one sweet girl could bring back all the bad-boy tendencies hiding deep inside me? I've done a great job of forgetting where I came from, and who I was, and all the fucked-up trouble I used to get into before I left home and came here to start over in college.

It was a lot of luck, but it was a lot of hard work too.

But the past is tattooed on my soul and on my body, so there's no way to leave all that shit behind.

And what the fuck is up with Ozzy bringing up Kenner and his band? Seriously have not even thought about that guy in over a decade. And tonight, the one night I would very much like to keep all my secret past transgressions buried, I not only have to acknowledge them, I have to make a fucking phone call to Kenner McConnell and beg him to meet someone's daughter when they play here in the summer. And to top it all off—as if this situation couldn't get any worse— Amherst invited Ozzy and me to his country club Spring Fling in two weeks so he can introduce us to all his friends.

Which means we *have* to go.

At exactly eight forty-five I go down to the garage, get in my car, and drive over to the co-op. It's nine on the dot when I walk through the door and I'm surprised by two things.

One, Aria is in her cube. And two, so is that pesky ballerina.

Like, seriously? The universe can't cut me one break? I know I told Aria I'd be here tonight—practically invited her to meet me—but after meeting her father, who I realize I genuinely like, not to mention respect, it was a horrible idea.

And I can't even talk to her the way I want, because I'm certain the ballerina has a thing for me. She's been hanging out all fucking week trying to make me notice her.

I pass by Aria's cube and accidentally make eye contact with her. We both look away quickly. But then I remember I have my test results in my back pocket and

139

pull out the envelope and hold it up for her to see through the glass.

She pushes back from her computer and opens the door.

"Here you go," I say. "Also…" I glance down the hallway where the ballerina—what the fuck is her name? I feel stupid calling her the ballerina—is watching us. "Just… yeah. It was nice meeting your father today. He seems like a really good guy."

She stares at me for a moment. Then the envelope. Then me again. "Thanks," she says, taking it from my hand. "I really wasn't that worried about it."

"Well…" Yeah, I got nothing for that. "OK. See you around."

I turn back to the hallway, wave a hello finger at the ballerina, go inside my cube, and close the door behind me. I kick off my shoes and walk over to my kit, grabbing my sticks off the shelf.

The ballerina is directly across the hall from me. She's doing some exercise at her barre, pretending to be engrossed in her stretches, but glancing over at me every few seconds.

Aria is sitting back at her computer, leaning over. Probably reading my test results.

And how humiliating that is. Right? I was so irresponsible with her, I had to get tested to prove I'm not a man-whore with diseases.

She wasn't worried about it. I believe her. I wasn't either. I'm careful.

But the fact is… I fucked up.

I start pounding on my drums. Just making up a beat. My feet hitting the double bass as I bang out a clusterfuck of noise until I get a rhythm going. But my gaze is locked on Aria's cube. I want her to turn around. I want her to watch me. I want to put on a show for her.

I stop drumming and set my sticks down, then drag my t-shirt over my head and toss it on the floor. I want to make noise and work up a sweat. I want to push Aria Amherst up again a wall and finger her until she comes and then fuck her from behind until her legs are trembling and she's screaming my name.

But I can't. I can't ever touch her again.

So I just do the only thing I can. I play the drums and picture the way she so carefully sat down on my cock that night. The way she moaned, and squeaked when I was fully inside her. The evidence of what I did smeared all over my cock when we were done.

I live in the fantasy because Aria Amherst is now officially off limits.

141

CHAPTER THIRTEEN

After he walks away I stare at his back for a second and the way his tattoos move across the taut muscles of his arms and the way his biceps stretch when he lifts one hand to point at the ballerina girl, then again when he opens his door and walks inside.

The envelope is clutched in my fingers out in front of me and I turn, noticing the ballerina girl is now looking at me weird. Squinting her eyes a little. I sit back down at the computer. I came here under the pretense that I was going to touch up some photographs we were given in class today. But it was a lie.

I've been thinking about him all week. Every day when my dad comes to pick me up after class I secretly hope he's waiting there too. Fully understanding that it's a fantasy and having Ryker and my dad in the same vicinity is one of the worst ideas ever.

But then... earlier at dinner. My dad was happy and seemed to like Ryker. It was uncomfortable and weird, but the world didn't implode and I didn't catch on fire for not mentioning that, *Oh, hey. Small world, Dad. This older business guy you're doing deals with took my virginity in the most amazing way ever last weekend. It was the best night of my life.*

It *was* the best night of my life. I don't think I fully appreciated just how careful he was with me at the time. And that only made my tantrum about the truffle grilled cheese all that more ridiculous.

God. I really blew it. He's so done with me. And why shouldn't he be? I was acting like a child, that's why I felt like one. He wasn't treating me like a kid. He planned a pretty thorough adult sexual adventure for us and I messed it all up with my teenage insecurities.

I look at the letter in my hand. It's a very high-quality envelope. Thick and cream-colored. The kind my parents use when they're sending out party invitations. And across the front, written in red script Sharpie, is my name.

Aria. With a little flourish underneath.

Only the tip of the envelope flap has been secured, so a single finger inserted under it releases the seal.

I pull out a letter—same thick paper as the envelope—and two sheets of test results, which do, in fact, indicate that he has tested negative for all sexually transmitted diseases.

The letter is handwritten in the same script as my name.

Dear Aria,

I'm very sorry for making you worry about this. It was inappropriate and irresponsible. I hope this gives you some piece of mind and while I think you're a very lovely young woman, I'm afraid this is where we part ways. Again, I'm truly sorry for not being more careful, but I'm not sorry I met you.

I wish you all the best in the future.

Ryker

Well, shit. Now I feel horrible for making him do this. I feel horrible about all of it.

A cacophony of random drums fills the co-op and I glance over my shoulder and see him drumming.

I quickly glance back at my letter—tracing each handwritten word with my eyes.

His drumming stops, then starts again, and I chance one more look at him

Oh, fuck.

145

He took his shirt off and now he's got his eyes closed, getting into his music. The beat becomes rhythmic and steady.

The ballerina girl appears at my cube door, saying "Knock, knock," as she raps her knuckles in the air. I can't hear her over the drums, I just read her lips.

I wave her in and the door opens, the drums get louder, then she closes it behind her and it goes back down to a manageable level.

"Hey," she says. "You're April's sister, right?"

"Yup, that's me. I'm Aria."

"Nice to meet you Aria. I'm Babette."

Of course she is. *Babette*. That's got sexy ballerina written all over it.

"So… I was just wondering if you have a thing for him?"

"Who? What?" I say.

She nods her head in Ryker's direction. "That North guy. Because I like him and I'm pretty sure he likes me too. So… you know. I just didn't want you to be disappointed."

I squint my eyes at her. Fucking bitch. He is not into her. He's into me.

Or is he? Is that why we must part ways? So he can date the ballerina?

"How old are you?" I ask.

"Why?"

"Oh, I'm just curious. You're what? Twenty-two? Twenty-three?" I lowball.

She lifts her chin up and looks down her nose at me. "Twenty-seven."

"Ah," I say. "So do you dance professionally?"

"Why?" she asks.

"Oh, I'm just wondering. I used to dance ballet when I was younger." Really, I just want to be a bitch. Because I know what a defeated ballerina looks like. I took dance for ten years and almost all the girls in my classes had big dreams of dancing professionally. And every one of us—except one willowy, perfectly proportioned girl with the right genetics—was weeded out in our third or fourth year *en pointe*.

And this Babette here, she was one of the weeds.

I'm being mean. I know that. But she was mean first.

"I do theatre now," she says, stiffening.

"Cool," I say.

"Musicals," she adds.

"I love musicals," I say. "Let me know when you're in one. I'd love to come support you." I smile sweetly.

She smiles sweetly back. "I'll do that. Did he give you a note, or something?" she asks, looking down at my letter.

I fold it up, thankful I put his test results face down on the desk, and say, "Yeah. Just a thank you. We actually had dinner earlier. With my father," I clarify. "They do business together."

"Oh," she says. "So you know each other."

"Yeah, you could say that."

She nods. Then she turns on her toes—swear to God, on her toes—and walks out.

I sigh and give up. That was mean. I'm not usually a mean person. My dad always taught my sister and me that being mean is easy. Insulting people takes far less effort than being understanding and nice. And sure, it feels good in the moment but then you feel guilty. And if you're mean to people enough times, you become used to defending yourself with nastiness. And then one day you wake up and realize that good, sweet person you thought you were is gone.

Then he would look at us—mostly April, because she has an inherent mean streak towards people she dislikes—and say, "I know you're not that person. And I want the world to know you the way I do."

So… yeah. I feel awful and want to go make up for it somehow. Tell Babette nice things and maybe try to be friends.

But when I turn around she's flicked off the lights in her cube and she's heading out the back door.

Good going, Aria. Your father would be so proud of what you've turned into this past week. Seven days outside his influence and I'm everything he never wanted me to be.

I stick the letter inside my purse, then flip off the light, lock up, and leave by the front door.

The whole way home I think about Ryker this afternoon. Not Ryker last weekend. But the way he was polite and mature today. And how that's kinda nice. And maybe also how I might need someone like that— someone like my father—in my autonomous adult life. Someone to remind me of who I am.

When I get home I go upstairs to find Felix lounging in the middle of the floor. Flicking his tail up and down all impatient and irritated. He likes me, but he misses April and I think he's lonely.

I think I'm lonely too. Being on my own isn't the fun I thought it would be. I like privacy and I certainly have that here. But I do miss living with other people and I'm actually glad my dad has been picking me up from class. I'm also starting to wonder if I should stay here for the next few weeks or just go home.

I flop on the couch and switch the TV on, just surfing channels to waste time until I'm tired enough to sleep. Wishing I had handled things with Ryker differently on Monday. Wishing he hadn't given up on me so easily.

Suddenly I'm too tired to bother with TV. I just want to sleep. I click it off and hear footsteps coming up the stairs outside the door.

Holy shit. Is it Ryker?

My heart starts to beat fast. Hope flooding my body.

Then a knock.

"Who is it?" I ask. Because if it's not him—

"It's Ryker North, Aria. I just... need a minute."

Just a minute? Why just a minute? What could this be about?

"Can you open the door, please? I promise, I won't take long."

I get up, walk over, and open the door. He's standing on the other side, still sweaty from drumming—but unfortunately for me, he has a shirt on—with disheveled hair and both hands pressed against my doorframe so he's leaning forward a little bit.

"Umm… hello."

He holds up a finger. "I just need to say two things, OK?"

"OK."

"First—I know I said this already, but I need to say it again. I'm sorry."

"Which part, exactly, are you sorry for?" Because I'm confused. Did he not want to be with me at all? Does he regret having sex with me? Because that's definitely not what I want to hear.

"I didn't treat you right."

"Oh," I say.

"I mean…" He lifts his eyebrows up. "I think I did treat you right on your birthday. I think I did everything right, actually. Maybe not getting all alpha on you while your parents were waiting in the car when you were in the co-op. But after. I think I did… I think…" He sighs and runs his fingers through his hair. "I really enjoyed that. Being with you and being considerate and careful for your first time. I hope you remember that night forever and it's not something you regret."

I open my mouth to say, *I certainly won't.* But he holds up a finger.

"One more thing, then that's it."

151

"OK."

"Would you like to go out on a date with me this weekend?"

"A... date?"

"Yes. A real date. I pick you up on Friday night, take you somewhere nice. Bring you home. That kind of thing."

"A date."

"Yes."

I start nodding my head. "OK. Yes. I'd like to go on a date with you."

"Great," he says. "That's it. It was very nice meeting you today. The real you, I mean. And your father seems as easy to like as you are. So... Yeah. That's it. I'll pick you up at seven on Friday."

Then he turns and walks away.

"Ryker?" I say.

"Hmm?" He looks back at me over his shoulder.

"You don't want to come in?"

He shakes his head. "No. We're going to do this right. I'll see you Friday."

Then he disappears down the stairs and I close my door, leaning my back against it as I take all that in.

A real date. As in… we might be starting something real. We might be starting a relationship.

I think I swoon a little.

CHAPTER FOURTEEN

All week I've been asking myself, *Am I doing the right thing? Should I just back off and leave her alone? Is this wrong?*

And all week I've come up with answers on both sides. Is taking her out on a new first date the right thing? Probably not. It's a professional risk at this point. But I ask myself another question. If we weren't putting this deal together with her father, would I feel the same way? Yes and no. Because yes, I still want to ask her out. And no, I wouldn't be feeling this guilt over it.

If Aria were just some random eighteen-year-old girl I met in the co-op I'd still have that initial she's-too-young-for-me response. But after knowing her a week it would've faded. I feel that to be true.

It's only her father who gives me pause. And yet it was meeting him, and seeing her with him, that changed my mind that night I asked her out.

She is special. Not just special the way a father thinks his daughter is special, but in other ways too.

She kissed him on the cheek before she left. He gave her an heirloom diamond ring instead of a car for her birthday.

There are real familial ties at work here. And I like that. I love it, actually. Because that's not anything I've ever had before. I have Ozzy. He's my only family these days. But it's not the same. A business partnership isn't like a love relationship. And sure, I love the guy. I'd do anything for him and he'd do anything for me.

It's just not the same. I need more than that.

And her father seems to like us. Ozzy, because everyone loves Ozzy. But me too. He's dropped by our office twice this week because he was in the neighborhood for meetings. He's excited about our project and both times he's reminded us of the Spring Fling at the country club.

I feel like this is a good sign. That one day, if Aria and I continue to see each other, I could go to him and explain how I feel about his daughter and he'll understand. He'll get it. He'll get *us* and everything will work out.

If that vibe wasn't there I wouldn't have done it. I wouldn't have asked her out again.

But it was. So I did.

Is it wrong to date someone seventeen years younger than you?

Probably. But by whose standard? She's a legal adult. And even though this started out as a one-night stand, that's not what it is now. We stumbled a little that first weekend but we took time to think and fate brought us back together.

I feel like we've been given a second chance. A do-over.

So what if people look at us funny? Does it matter what they think if I love her?

Not that I love her. I don't love her. She doesn't love me. This is all totally in the like department… for now.

But if we did fall in love, then who's to say that it's wrong?

Ultimately no one gets to decide that but us. Her and me. And I've already decided it's not wrong. Not if you love someone. Not if you're doing it for the right reasons. So I'm going to make sure she knows I'm doing this because I want her.

I want to get to know her. I want to see the young woman her father sees. The innocent one. The sweet one.

"Jesus," Ozzy says. "What the hell are you daydreaming about? All week you've been distracted."

He sits on the corner of my desk. "What's going on with you?"

I take a deep breath and let it out. "You remember that girl I was telling you about?"

"Which one?"

"The last one," I say, rolling my eyes. "The young one."

"You mean," he says, raising one eyebrow at me, "the eighteen-year-old baby?"

"She's not a baby. She's an adult. And she's interesting. And good. I like her."

"Oh, shit," he says, rubbing his hand across his jaw. "Who is she?"

"I'm not ready to go there just yet. But maybe soon. If this all works out. I'm taking her out tonight. Real first date kinda thing," I say.

"Ah, man," he says, dropping a folder onto my desk.

"What?"

"Real first date? Like you just threw away the one-night stand and decided to start over? What the hell? Are you falling for this girl? Because I gotta say, that's not a good idea, Ryker. Age difference. It never works out. Cut your losses, dude. She's gonna shatter you. I mean, eighteen? She hasn't even lived yet and you…" He shakes his head. "You've lived a little too much."

I've lived a little too much.

Not untrue, either. I've got the figurative scars and literal tattoos to prove it.

"And what's up with this drummer stuff? I've asked you to come out and have drinks with me all week and every time you blow me off for the fucking drums. What gives? What's going on?"

"I like it," I say. "I miss it. I guess I didn't realize how much until I started playing again."

"So… do you miss the old you too? Because I gotta tell ya, Ryker, I didn't care for that guy much. I certainly didn't go into business with him. And I know I brought up your friend in the band, but I was just showing off for Amherst. You know how I feel about old you."

"No," I say. "I swear. It's nothing like that. I just miss the energy, ya know? The music, the—"

"The lifestyle," he interrupts. "Is that why you're dating this younger girl? You've clawed your way to the top of the food chain and now you're missing all the things you left behind?"

"That's not why."

"You sure about that, buddy? Because I'm no therapist, but this is what you'd call a classic mid-life crisis. If you were married you'd be getting a divorce—"

"Fuck you," I say. "That's not even cool."

159

He shrugs and hold his hands up. "Callin' it like I see it, bro. Everyone else around here just sees you as you are now. But me?" He shakes his head. "I knew you before. I know why you did the things you did and fucked shit up."

"And it was you who pulled me out of it in sophomore year of college, I know, I know."

He points his finger at me. "Don't fuck this up, Ryker. You worked goddamned hard to put the past behind you and start over. Don't let misplaced nostalgia and the desire to be young again pull you off the rails. Fuck this girl. I mean, literally, fuck her brains out. Get it out of your system. But don't be naive. Don't let her innocence and fresh-faced youth lead you astray. It can't work. Everyone knows this."

"Yeah," I say. "Sure. You're right."

There's no sense arguing with Ozzy. Once he takes a position on something he won't back down. But that's OK. Aria and I need time to figure this out for ourselves before we make a public announcement. And hey, maybe he's right. Maybe it all crashes and burns tonight. No harm done.

And if he's wrong then by the time we do go public we'll be solid and no one will be able to break us apart.

He leans across my desk, clasps me on the shoulder, and says, "Good talk, brother. It's the right decision. You wanna come have drinks with me and Tiffany tonight?"

"Who is Tiffany?" I ask.

"Never mind," he says, standing up and laughing. "Next week it'll be someone else, so why waste my breath. Have fun drumming," he adds, walking out of my office.

I breathe a sigh of relief when he says goodbye to the staff and leaves. I love me some Ozzy, but I don't want to hear his opinions about Aria and me.

I decide to leave early too. But before I go I text her. Just to make sure she's hasn't forgotten. Even though I've been in the co-op every night this week, she's been absent. I text her once a day. Just one time to say I hope she had a nice day. And each time she's texted me back with an answer and asked about mine.

It's kinda… sweet.

Goddamn, everything about her is sweet.

My fingers flash across my phone as I write, *See you at seven. And don't wear a dress.*

It's delivered. Read. And typing bubbles appear immediately. I hope that's her excited response and not an oh-shit-I-forgot-to-cancel response.

Yes, I love her youth. I am distracted by her fresh face and innocence. That's precisely why I've decided to take this relationship seriously and super-slow.

We're gonna get to know each other. We're gonna bond. We don't need sex to do that.

Her reply pops up with a ding.

Don't wear a dress? How will you finger me in the car?

Oh, shit. I think I just got hard.

A winking emoji pops up. Then a bitmoji picture of her avatar pouting with the caption "y tho" over her head.

Bitmojis. I just smile. Because OK, yeah. She makes me feel young again. Everything that's happened since the moment I first saw her in that board meeting has made me feel alive again.

I text back, *You'll see. Jeans and a t-shirt, please.* And then *#trustme.*

She sends me another bitmoji of her blowing a heart-shaped kiss that says *See you soon!*

But now I'm hopelessly distracted by the thought of fingering her in the car.

CHAPTER FIFTEEN

First of all, he picks me up in a limo. A limo. Not the company car with a driver. Which is also swanky and cool, but not nearly as romantic as a limo. That's my first clue that this is gonna be a very different kind of date than the first time at the Corinthian.

The second clue is that he brings me flowers. Actually, a single red rose. Long-stemmed and already in a crystal bud vase.

"First time," I tell him as he smiles at my reaction. "First time a man has brought me flowers."

I don't tell him that Larry picked me some daisies at summer camp two years ago because Larry didn't even get his skinny little dick inside me so he loses all chances at any firsts forever.

Ryker smiles and nods. Not even one lewd comment about how he's gonna take all my firsts. And then I picture giving him my first blow job. Because we haven't gotten there yet and I'm wondering if tonight is the night.

So then we go downstairs and get in the limo and I have no idea where we're going, but I'm pretty disappointed that his fingers aren't inside me. But of course, I'm wearing jeans so that's a whole production I knew we weren't going to deal with.

But the date is a local rock band at a little venue in mid-town. Eighteen and up, so even though Ryker is clearly over twenty-one, they won't sell him alcohol because we have different-colored wrist bands. When I realize that I feel a little embarrassed that he had to take me to a place like this. How long has it been since he's had a night out with a woman that doesn't involve drinks?

So I ask him if he wants me to go stand somewhere else so he can get a drink and he says, "I didn't bring you here to drink, Aria. We can drink anywhere we want. I brought you to see the band."

Which, I admit, kinda makes me like him a little more in that moment.

And if Ryker feels self-conscious about being one of the older dudes among all the twenty-somethings, he doesn't show it. He holds my hand and leads me through the crowd. When people get rowdy near us, he stands in front of me and dares them to take another step forward. When the music comes on he finds us a spot near the front and wraps his arms around me like a protector.

There isn't much talking but for some reason it works for us. I get the opportunity to relax, and people-watch, and listen to the music. I've never been to one of these shows before. There are a few kids in my school who are into this scene. All-ages clubs, and drinking, and pot. But honesty, St. Bernadette's is a little microcosm of the city where none of the bad stuff exists. Maybe that's stupid. Maybe keeping kids sheltered like this is just wishful thinking. But I like being safe and if I was here alone tonight I'd be terrified. Ryker takes away all the apprehension about trying new things and just lets me exist. There are no expectations other than that. It's an opportunity to appreciate things for the first time in a safe way.

Kinda like the way he took my virginity.

And when I go back to high school in a week none of my friends will even believe the time I had over break. I feel like a whole different person. The sex, the college class, the apartment, the co-op… I feel like Aria Amherst got dropped off somewhere and this new, adult version of me took over.

Now I glance over at Ryker in the back of the limo. I'm stretched out on the back seat with my feet in his lap and he's massaging them because I was dumb and wore heels. And while this was just some local band, they were pretty popular tonight and we had to stand the whole time.

But back to Ryker North.

Mmmmm. He looks delicious in his jeans and t-shirt. It's an old, once-black-but-now-faded-to-gray concert shirt. That band that April always loved. Son of a Jack.

He's looking intently at my feet as he rubs my toes and I'm watching the tattoos on his arms dance with his movements. Demons, all of them. Red and black with swirls of smoke and flames.

He glances over at me and says, "Did you have fun tonight?"

I nod my head slowly. "I did. Never been to a show before. And the only concerts I've gone to are the ones my parents took me to. And that was all classical music."

He smiles and laughs.

"You probably think I'm so young, don't you. So inexperienced and innocent."

"Those aren't bad things to be, Aria."

"I know, but… you can't even drink around me without people suspecting you of corruption. It didn't bother you?"

He shakes his head and frowns. "No." Then he looks over at me, his hair falling over his eyes. "I feel responsible for you," he says. "Especially after meeting your father. Maybe that first night I went home thinking, you know. *Not for me*. But I've changed my mind, Aria. You are for me."

I think about that for a few moments. "So that's what this was? Our first date."

"Yeah. This was a good first date. No awkward conversation, no expectations, no ulterior motives."

"Whoa, hold on," I say, putting a hand up to indicate full stop. "I hope you're not planning on dropping me off and kissing me good night at the door."

He smiles, still massaging my toes. "That was the plan."

"Uh… no," I say. "Just noooo." And I pout a little. "I want to see your house. You've seen a whole bunch of me and I haven't seen anything of you. It's not fair."

He considers this and says, "Fair enough. You want to see my apartment?"

"Yes."

He leans forward enough to tab the controls for the blacked-out divider separating us from the driver and lowers it. "Change of venue, we're going back to my place."

"Yes, sir, Mr. North," the driver says.

Then Ryker raises the divider and leans back again.

"Is this your limo?" I ask. Because I figured he rented it.

"Company limo. Same driver as usual, though."

"Oh." So interesting. My father is rich. I think. I guess. I always thought we were rich. But unless he's going to the airport he drives himself everywhere. Even when I used to have dance classes, or art classes, or that one year I took piano—he drove me everywhere. Always dropped me off. Always picked me up. So this company limo stuff is foreign to me.

"Do you think my father likes you?" I ask.

He gives me a sideways look out of the corner of his eye. "So far."

I chuckle a little. "Yeah, I don't know what he would think about this."

"I have a pretty good idea. That's why I'm trying to do this right, Aria. His opinion is important, and not because we're in the middle of a deal. His opinion is important because..." He runs his hand through his hair again, sighing. "Well, because he loves you. It's pretty clear you're his sweet princess of a daughter. And if I have any hope of seeing you long-term, his opinion of me matters."

Long-term. "I'm sorry, did you just say long-term? Or am I hearing things?"

He does that side-eye thing again. "Unless you don't want to see me long-term. I might be getting ahead of myself."

"You want to see me long-term? As in... after spring break is over? After April comes back and kicks me out of her apartment? After my life goes back to normal?"

"Like I said, unless you don't want to."

I just stare at him for a few seconds. Blinking in astonishment. Then manage to say, "I guess it never occurred to me."

"Which part?"

"That you would actually... care about me."

"It took me by surprise as well. But I do. I like you, Aria. And if keeping your attention means making sure you have all the right experiences in all the right order, then that's what I'm prepared to do."

"But... we're going to have sex tonight, right?"

He laughs. And his smile is big. And that's when I realize—he hasn't smiled much tonight. He was pretty serious, in fact. Still is. "We'll see," he says.

But now I'm thinking about him instead of me. "Did you have fun tonight?"

"Are you kidding?"

"No, I'm serious. Because you didn't smile much."

"Oh." He smiles again. "I was worried about you. People getting too close to you. Knocking you down

169

or spilling drinks on you. But I had a really good time doing that."

I think I swoon at that. Actually get a little light-headed.

"The whole point was to just take you out and show you something new. A little of me, I guess. So you're wrong, actually. I did show you me. And I hope you enjoyed the music because I did. I liked that band a lot."

I open my mouth to say something but the car stops and Ryker looks past me out my window. "This is me," he says, grabbing my heels and slipping them on my feet. Then he places them on the floor just as the driver opens my door.

I get out and he gets out after me. Then he nods to the driver and takes my hand, leading me to the front of his building.

The doorman greets him by name, then nods his head at me and says, "Good evening, ma'am," as he opens the door.

The lobby is almost empty so the only sound is the echo of our shoes tapping on the tiled floor. In the elevator he flashes a keycard at a sensor and the button for the penthouse lights up.

I glance at him, grinning, and he offers me a small, humble shrug.

At the top the doors open straight into his apartment.

Floor-to-ceiling views of midtown, large, gray, leather sectional sofa with two red accent chairs, and room-sized white rug over dark hardwood floors.

"I'm boring," he says. "I'm not here that much, so please don't judge my decorating."

He walks me over to the window and we stand there in silence for a few seconds. Then I look up at him and grin. "I don't think I understand you."

"What do you mean?"

I look at his reflection in the glass—his concert t-shirt, his faded jeans, his demon tattoos—then refocus so I can see the apartment behind him. Such a contrast. "Where did you come from, Ryker North? Not midtown. You didn't go to a school like St. Bernadette's, did you? So who are you?"

He sighs, drops my hand, and then walks over to a drink cart and begins pouring himself a drink from a decanter. Takes a sip. Looks at me. Takes another one. Sets the drink down.

I can't help but notice that he doesn't offer me one.

"It's a long story," he finally says.

I kick off my heels and walk over to him, unsure if I'm allowed to touch him, but unable to stop myself. So I place my hands on his arms and say, "I've got all night, Mr. North."

171

"But is that really how you want to spend it?" Then he winks. "Talking, Aria?"

"Hey," I say. "You were planning on kissing me goodnight at the door, remember?"

"I know what I was planning. I'm asking you what you were planning."

I blush. Immediately.

He runs his fingers through his hair for the hundredth time tonight. It's sexily disheveled.

"Well?" he asks, when my silence goes on too long.

"No," I admit. "I wasn't planning on talking tonight."

His hand finds my waist and he pulls me closer. "This is why I wanted to take you home. Believe me, I want to do all the things to you tonight. But I'm trying to be good and go slow."

I swallow hard, then say, "What if I don't want you to be good?"

CHAPTER SIXTEEN

I want to be strong, I really, really do. I want to go slow, and be careful with her, and show her that this isn't about sex, it's about us. That we're building something here. Something special, and unique, and I'm not just interested in her body.

But my hands have other ideas. My fingers are already slipping up inside her t-shirt, palms pressing flat on her breasts. She closes her eyes and leans into me.

"Aria," I say. Because she's driving me crazy.

"Don't be good," she says. "Please don't be good. I can't stop thinking about how it felt to have you inside me and how I could still feel you the next day."

"Fuck," I moan.

"I was so sore," she says. "It felt so weird, but so good, too. And I've been thinking about you. Playing that night over and over in my head. That's all I want,

Ryker. That's it. Just for you to be inside me again so I can feel that way."

I take a deep breath and pull her bra down under her shirt.

"I should've worn a dress. Then you wouldn't even have to take off my pants. I could just slip into your lap and—"

I pull her t-shirt over her head and she squeaks with surprise, giggling as I toss it over my shoulder. Her tits are big and bunched up from her bra.

"Get me naked," she says. "Take my clothes off and then I'll take off yours."

I reach around her back and unhook her bra. It falls down her arms and she flicks it to the floor at her bare feet.

I just look at her for a moment. Her long, dark, red hair is flowing over her shoulders. And she has some makeup on so her eyes are darker than normal. She is sweet, but tonight she looks dark too. Dark and hungry.

I picture my cock in her mouth. How she'll gag on it. And how that'll make me feel and I suddenly want to forget I'm supposed to be careful and just bend her over and fuck her in the ass.

Calm down, Ryker. Calm down.

"Here," she says, placing my fingers at the button of her jeans. "Let me help you."

Where did she learn to talk like this?

But then I realize… she's not even dirty-talking to me. She's just being helpful and truthful. Just being innocent and young.

I'm going to hell for this. I'm corrupting her and there's no way karma won't get me back for that.

But those are thoughts for another time. I pop the button on her jeans and pull her zipper down. Slide my hand between her legs as I turn her around and hold her close to my chest.

"I want your fingers inside me," she says. "I like that. I like that a lot."

I rub her clit though her panties and she grips my wrist, urging me to put my fingers inside her.

I want to talk back to her. Make her as hot as she's getting me, but I can't fucking think straight. My cock is pressing against my jeans, so hard and ready for her. And my mind is clouded with lust and desire to do exactly what she tells me.

She's so wet her sweet liquid seeps through her panties. That's my excuse for holding all the dirty things in. She doesn't need it. But I don't either and I still like it.

So I say, "You know what I liked about you that night?"

"Hmmm?" she asks. "What?"

"I liked how your tight pussy clamped down on my cock when you came. I wanted to come inside you so bad."

"I thought about how you came on my tits that night. How it was sticky. And then I wondered what it would taste like."

"Jesus Christ, Aria. You're telling me you want to swallow?"

She turns to face me, places both her hands on either side of my face, and says, "I've never had a cock in my mouth and I want you to be the first. I want you to be all my firsts."

Then her fingers are popping the button on my jeans and my hands are rubbing her ass, my fingers still slick with her juice as I slip them back between her legs from behind and give her asshole a little rub.

"Even here?" I ask, my eyes fixed on hers as she takes out my cock and begins squeezing it.

She doesn't answer. Which means... she knows guys like to fuck girls in the ass. And she probably knows some girls like it, too. But she's not sure.

"Don't worry," I say. "We can save that for another night."

"Take off my pants. I want to be naked this time. No teasing me this time. Just… put yourself inside me."

"Patience," I say, smiling. "You have to come at least once before I do that."

"Why?" She pouts.

"Because I want you to be dripping wet when I slide up inside you."

She reaches down, slipping her hand between her legs. Then she pulls her fingers out, glistening and shiny. She places them up to my lips and says, "I'm already there."

I grab her hand and shove her finger in my mouth, licking it and sucking it as she helps me wiggle her jeans over her hips and then starts pushing them down her legs with her foot.

I laugh, still holding her fingers up to my mouth.

"What's so funny?"

But I just shake my head. "You're too fucking cute, you know that?"

"I want my pants off, dammit!" We both laugh. "And you're not going fast enough."

"Torture is sweet, sweet thing," I say.

"Hold on," she says, then sits down on the floor in front of me and begins tugging her skinny jeans down over her feet. She's flashing her soaking wet panties at me, legs open and knees bent as she contorts on the ground until finally, she throws her jeans off to the side.

"There," she says, propping herself up with her hands as she leans back. Her knees are bent and pressed together. But as soon as she sees me looking at them, she opens them up wide. Until her thighs are flat on the tiled floor. She doesn't smile. Just takes one hand and slips her fingers under her panties and then she pulls them aside for me.

Her sweet pussy is pink and glistening as she begins to play with herself as I watch. Stunned motionless. Unable to take my eyes off her.

"Condoms," I say, suddenly remembering.

She shakes her head. "No. I want to feel you."

Where the hell did this girl come from? How the hell did I ever get so lucky? And then... yeah. That test was a good idea after all.

"Hey," I say, reaching down. "Come here." She takes my hand and I pull her to her feet. "You wanna try another first tonight?"

She nods her head and starts tugging on my jeans. But I stop her and say, "No. I'm gonna leave them on. I'm gonna fuck you with my pants on. Like we're doing it in a stairwell at work. Or up in your childhood bedroom with your parents downstairs. Like we're having a hot quickie, but it won't be quick."

She sucks in a breath of air. "Is that my new first?"

"No," I say, shaking my head. "I want to fuck up against the window."

She looks over her shoulder, then back at me. "OK."

"You sure about that?"

"Why wouldn't I be sure?"

"Because we're in the city and people spy through windows with telescopes."

"People can see us?" she asks, turning to face the window.

"Maybe. You never know."

She turns back to me and says, "I'm sure. Let them look." She backs up against the window, arms stretched wide like she's offering herself to me.

But I shake my head at her. "Not quite."

She furrows her brow. "Then how?"

I reach down and lift her up. Rubbing her pussy against the shaft of my hard cock. "Like this," I say. "Now put me inside you."

She sucks in air, nodding as she reaches down, wraps her little hand around my thick cock, and points it at her pussy.

One good fuck isn't enough to make this easy. One good fuck doesn't let me slide right in. So she winces and gasps as I push my head inside her. Fingernails gripping my shoulders as I press her back against the glass and ease my hips forward.

"Ow," she says.

"I'll stop," I reply. "Just say the word and—"

"Don't stop," she moans. "Do it fast and hard. I know it'll feel good once you're fully inside me."

I don't hesitate. I thrust forward hard and quick, just like she asked me to, her legs wrapped around my hips, squeezing me tight.

I wait like that for a few seconds as she breathes heavy and hard. Then, when I know she's gotten use to my big size, I pull back, just a little, just enough so I can thrust forward again.

Again she says, "Ow." Just one more tiny ow. And the next time she moans. And the time after that, she hisses. And the time after that she reaches down and begins playing with herself.

"Yeah," I say. "Yes. Make yourself come and then I'll give you another first. I'll put my cock between your lips. Just a little. Just a little taste—"

"Oh, God," she says. "Oh, God."

"Just the tip, Aria. You can't have all of it at once."

"I want it all," she says, leaning her forehead on my shoulder. Her body is limp except for her legs and her fingers. Just limp as I hold her up against the glass and slowly fuck her hard so that each thrust forward she has to exhale because I'm forcing the breath from her lungs.

"I want to be on top of you," she says. "I want to come on top of you."

I swing her around, mission accomplished with the window, and walk her over to the couch. I sit and lie back a little, still holding her, still inside her, and say, "Ride me, sweet thing. Rub that pussy all over me."

She places both her hands on my chest, her long hair hanging down and covering her face. And she begins to move. I grip her hips, guiding her just a little. She's rubbing her pussy on me. Trying to stimulate her clit. For a girl who's never fucked before she met me, she sure knows how to please herself.

The idea that I could be falling in love with a natural sexual deviant makes me feel like I won the lottery. Like we have years and years of dirty sex ahead of us.

"Jesus," I say, making myself even more turned on thinking about our future.

"I think I'm going to come."

181

"Do it," I say. "Do it. Come all over my dick."

She goes stiff for a second, her eyes wide. And then her fingernails grip into my chest as she arches her back and wails. Her pussy contracts around my shaft and I almost blow. It takes every fucking year of experience I have not to come inside her right now.

I need this girl on the pill. Soon. Because I want to feel that. I want to come with her and I can't.

She slumps forward, exhausted. Her knees pressing against my ribs as she buries her head into my neck and breathes hard.

I rub her ass cheeks. Slowly caressing her. My fingers slipping down between her legs to push against her tightly puckered asshole. My cock still rock hard inside her.

"Now you," she says, a few moments later. "Now you put it in my mouth."

Holy fuck. "Are you sure?"

She twirls a finger on my bare chest and says, "Mmmm-hmmmmm," so it comes out like a slow seductive moan.

"Then get on your knees in front of the couch."

She lifts herself off me. My dick slowly sliding out of her pussy. It falls forward, slapping against my stomach as she gets down on the floor and I swing my legs around so she's boxed in by my knees.

I fist my wet and glistening cock and say, "OK, but you have to go slow. And you only get to suck the tip."

"What? Is that how it's done?"

Sweet, sweet child.

"For you, this time, it is. Trust me. That's all it'll take."

Just the thought of her pouty, plump lips touching my cock makes me want to come.

She leans forward with her mouth open. Her eyes only on my cock. I say, "Eyes up here, sweetie." And she looks at me, smiling as I press the very tip of my cock up to her lips. She wraps them around the head, taking the whole swollen knob into her mouth, then gags and pulls back.

"Sorry," she says.

"Don't be," I reply. "This is the very best part. Now do it again."

She opens again, and again she takes the whole head and pulls back gagging.

"I'm sorry." She frowns.

"Aria," I say. "I want to come on your face just watching you do that. Now do it again. And keep doing it. I don't even want you to take me deep. This is all I want."

She wraps her hands around my shaft and leans in again. And this time I lean back on the couch and free my balls from the constriction of my jeans.

Tips of lips, then gagging.

The blood is pumping and rushing inside my cock. A burst of warmth, then pure heat as pressure inside me builds and builds, each time she puts her hot mouth over my skin. And each time she gags, it builds higher and higher.

I grab her head, forcing her to stay in place as she sucks on the tip of my dick. Not really struggling or make me back off, but letting me control her.

"If you don't want me to come in your mouth, back off now, Aria. Because I'm going to."

She doesn't back off. Just gags a little more and that's all I can take. That's all the self-control I have. I ease my hips down towards the edge of the couch so I've got her head directly over the top of me, and I let it out with a pulsing gush of relief.

She gags, and spits, and pulls back.

I hold on to her for one more second. Just one more second and then… release.

"Shit," I mumble. "Holy fucking shit." I open my eyes and look at her. Come dripping over her lips as she stares at me.

"Come here," I say, pulling her up into my lap. "This is what you do afterward."

I swipe the come off her face with my fingers and press them up to her lips. She opens, unsure what to do.

"Lick it," I say. "Lick it off my fingers."

And she does.

CHAPTER SEVENTEEN

He holds me after we're done. Just holds me in his arms on the couch. I have never felt so loved in my life. Even though almost everything we just did was new and scary, it was thrilling and worth it.

All of it. All of my firsts with him.

We spend the weekend together but also apart. I wanted to sleep over that night but he said no. He wanted to take me home. But would I be interested in going on a date tomorrow night?

We did go out on Saturday. He took me to a movie and we ate popcorn and laughed, and had fun. But the real fun was when he took me home to his apartment and we tried more new things. I sat on his face and he ate me until I came all over it. And he stuck his finger in my ass once too. I came immediately when he did that and he called me a dirty little deviant whom he never wanted to let go.

Then he took me home again. Firm in the belief that we will date and not play house, as he called it. Date. Because he wanted me to experience dating.

Then the weekend was over and I went back to class, and he went back to work, and we didn't see each other all week. Just talked on the phone every night before bed until the weekend rolled around and we went on dates again.

On Friday he took me to dinner and even though I wore a skirt, much to my disappointment, he didn't finger me under the table.

"No more of that right now," he said. "One day we'll play those games again, but not now."

At first I complained. I didn't understand. But he said, "I want to do this right, Aria." And that's all I needed to hear.

After dinner we went to his place again and we tried out some bondage. Just me tied to his bed with silk scarves. He left the room for what seemed like ages. Left me naked and horny. Craving him as he watched TV and had a drink.

And when he came back I was desperate for him. So desperate all he had to do was stick one finger inside me and I gushed.

He said one day, if I'm a very good girl, he'll show me what men really do to women tied to their beds.

I wanted to try immediately, but he said no. Just... one day.

That Saturday we went to the horse races and he let me pick all his bets, then went to the counter to place them. We ate lunch in the clubhouse and won sixty dollars on my picks.

That night he took me home and asked me if I'd ever watched porn before.

No. But I wanted to. So he put some on and asked which ones made me want to fuck him.

All of them, I decided. All of them. He had a toy to put in my butt that night. A crystal plug made for beginners. Because he said he could tell I'd like it. But he had to do it right or I wouldn't come back for seconds. He fucked me with that in my ass. Twice. And both times I came instantly.

I got on the pill too. He took me to a doctor Friday afternoon and waited outside while I had my exam, and

I came out with a prescription that we filled together at the drugstore nearby. He can't come inside me without a condom yet—which I do not want to use—but soon, he promised. Soon we'll have that first together too.

And then spring break was over and so was my Photoshop class. I went back in to high school with a Photoshop certificate that counted as credit and a sore pussy from my magical two weeks with a thirty-five-year-old man.

While all my friends chatted and talked about their tropical vacations with their parents, I daydreamed about what it would feel like to have Ryker's cock in my ass. I got myself so worked up I went into the bathroom during calculus, braced myself again the stall wall, and rubbed my clit through my panties until I came.

And all afternoon I smelled my desire for him as I sat at my desk pretending to be interested in American literature.

My father picked me up every day after school and took me to early dinner before dropping me off at home. And every day I wondered what he'd think of this. How he'd react if he knew what Ryker North was doing to me on the weekends. What I was doing to him. What we were doing to each other.

But one afternoon I decided to tell him about it. Well, a little bit. "I met a boy," I said in the car.

"You did?" My father beamed at me. "What's his name and who are his parents?"

I laughed. *If you only knew, Dad.* "I'm on the wait-and-see path before I make this public, Dad. You understand, right?"

And he had the perfect response. Because he said, "Whatever makes you happy, sweetie."

I really think, that when, one day, Ryker and I decide we're getting married, he will be happy for us. Because I'm falling for Ryker. I'm falling for him hard and while it's important to me that my family like him as much as I do, when it all comes down to it I honestly don't care.

Childhood is over and my life belongs to me now.

If Ryker wanted to make sure we go "long-term", as he put it, by going slow and fast at the same time—well, mission accomplished. Because he's all I think about. Day and night, I crave his fingers, and his mouth, and his cock.

And on the night before April comes back from Australia and I have to go live at home I decide something. I make a decision.

I love Ryker North and I want to be with him forever.

I want him to come inside me and I want him to do that someplace very special.

CHAPTER EIGHTEEN

I was afraid things would change once Aria went back to high school, but they really didn't. Once I decided that this was real for me and I was going to take my time, I did everything right. I made myself stay away during the week so she could concentrate on her own life. I forbade her from seeing me at the co-op and made strict rules about how much we could talk on the phone.

Just ten minutes each night before bed.

I don't want to take over her life. I don't want her to ignore her friends or her schoolwork. I don't want to be the only thing she has. I just want to be there when she expects me and when she needs me.

And I want to get this out in the open. I just don't know how. And I would never say anything to Ozzy or her father unless we talked it through first, and we're not there yet. So. Limbo. I feel like we're in limbo.

This is why I like the dates. We're not hiding out at her sister's apartment or my place. We're doing things and going places. It's important for me, and for her too, that we do not treat this as a secret.

The second challenge was her returning to her parents' house in the suburbs. Because there's no way to deny the fact that this is a secret and we are sneaking around because now I can't just pick her up for a date. She has to make an excuse to go into the city on Friday night. Or Saturday, but not both. Both is too much. And even though she's eighteen and we both know she's eighteen, she's in high school. She lives with her parents. She's not really an adult yet.

So now I'm conflicted.

But today is the Spring Fling at her father's country club and both Ozzy and I are going. Our loan package is almost complete. We finalize the last phase in the Gingerbread redevelopment project on Monday. And I'm having this internal dilemma about signing those papers while hiding the fact that I'm dating Mr. Amherst's teenage daughter.

There's just something about this that runs deep for me.

My phone dings a text and it's Ozzy: *Downstairs now with the car.*

I text back: *Be right there.*

Once last sigh and then I tuck away my guilt and get in the elevator.

The ride out to the Amherst country club takes almost an hour. They live in a very upscale neighborhood with massive homes, large, green lawns, and a gate around the entire place.

The Spring Fling is a horse show and golf tournament for the kids of the neighborhood. Aria neither rides nor plays golf, so for her, it's just a high-end block party.

She already told me that most of the kids she lives around go to school locally and only she and her sister commuted to the city for school. She didn't really know why, but I did.

Mr. Amherst loves his family and he probably felt like working in the city and living in the suburbs would take a lot of time away from him and his daughters. He enrolled them into a school near work so he could have commute time with them. Aria already told me her mother didn't work a regular job, but instead sat on the country club board and was in charge of the various parties and functions. And she stayed home with them when they were little, driving them to and from their various classes until they left for school in the city in high school.

I admire their division of parental labor. I truly do. Because I could imagine it was hard for Aria's mother to give up being more involved in her girls' lives so her husband could have his turn too.

And that just makes this whole thing even more agonizing.

They are the perfect family. They love each other, they are committed to one another, and they put the good of the family unit above personal need.

And when they find out their eighteen-year-old daughter is dating me—well, that's going to rip them apart.

I don't want to do that. I really don't.

But I won't give her up. I know she's off limits but I just do not care.

I think I'm falling in love with Aria Amherst.

"Are you even listening to me?" Ozzy says.

"Hmm?" I say, dragging my eyes of the view outside my window to stare at him.

"I just asked you about that house on State Street."

"What about it now?"

"What is up with you?"

"What do you mean?"

"You're so fucking distracted these days. Oh," he says. "Oh, no."

"What?"

"It's that young one, right? You're still dating that young one, aren't you? I've asked you to come out with me and Danielle twice over the past two weeks and I just get flat nos."

"Which one is Danielle again?"

"Funny," he says. Then he opens his mouth to question me more, but thankfully we pull to a stop in front of the country club and he gets distracted. "Well, all right now. This is some setup right here. Reminds me of home." He sighs.

"Yeah, me too," I joke. "Horse shows and golf tournaments have always been my thing."

Ozzy side-eyes me. "What's gotten in to you, man?"

"Nothing," I say, opening my door and stepping out. "I'm good. Let's go drink some good whiskey and smoke cigars like assholes."

"I'm in." Ozzy laughs. "Let's go."

We walk up to the front of the club and immediately spy Mr. and Mrs. Amherst wearing spring fashion— light-colored linen suit for the Mr. and pale peach dress for the Mrs.—as they chat up their neighbors in the lobby.

"Oh, Mr. Herrington. Mr. North. So happy you could make it." He extends his hand to each of us, then introduces his wife.

But I'm not looking at his wife.

I'm looking at his daughter. Because Aria Amherst appears through a set of double doors coming out of the garden party tent looking like a sweet little thing who has fucking on her mind.

CHAPTER NINETEEN

"Come here, Aria," my father says. "Remember Mr. Herrington and Mr. North?"

"I sure do," I say, beaming at Ryker's partner Ozzy, then at Ryker. He looks so nice today. Light gray slacks, a tan button-down shirt with no tie, and a short gray jacket. I have an urge to walk over to him and straighten his lapels, then kiss him on the cheek.

Such an urge to touch him right now.

"Nice to see you again," Ozzy says.

"You as well," I say. "But if you'll excuse me, I'm going out to the barn to look at the horses. I've always loved show day when they're all prettied up."

I smile at Ryker one last time, then turn, making sure my short spring dress twirls, and walk back outside to the barns. Hoping Ryker will meet me out there soon.

It's not soon, but Ryker does eventually show up. Poking his head into stalls and asking questions of all the girls showing today.

They swoon over him instantly and that makes me proud, not jealous. So I wait my turn, trying my best to be patient, as he makes his way down the shed row towards the bench I'm sitting on.

"Nice club you have here, Miss Amherst."

"Why, thank you, Mr. North. But you should see the house."

He grins, then shakes his head and looks down at the ground as he sticks his hands in his pockets. "I don't think so, Aria."

"Why?" I ask, all pouty and sad. "There's a path through the woods right there." I point to the blacktop path. "And on the other end is my backyard. Don't you want to see my bedroom?"

He looks around, nervous. "Not today, sorry."

"OK," I say. "But I'm going home now. I need a nap."

And then I do the flirty turn again and begin walking towards the path in the woods. I get just out of sight and then I wait, ducking behind a tree.

He sees me once he rounds the bend. "This is a bad idea."

"We could go back." I shrug. Like I'm not dying to take him up to my room. But I am, of course. It's going to be very hard to see him anymore. I can't just make excuses to go into the city every weekend. This might be my one chance for weeks. Hell, I might not see him until I move into the dorms for college in the fall. I can't waste this chance.

"Aria." He sighs. "You're killing me." But then he extends his hand, and I take it, and we walk through the woods like a couple. Like a real couple.

My house is only a ten-minute walk from the club house and we spend that time catching up on our week. He's been busy with the redevelopment project, I've been busy with getting ready for finals. And just when I think he's the height of self-control and this afternoon won't turn out the way I planned, he pushes me behind a tree and kisses me on the mouth.

"Oh, God," I moan into our kiss. "I've missed you so much this week."

His hand slides underneath my skirt and finds that spot between my legs that drives me wild.

"I want your fingers inside me," I beg.

"Let's go inside," he says. "Show me your room."

I reluctantly back away and take his hand, pulling him. He hesitates, but only for a moment. Then we are practically running through my back yard. Past my old play set. Past my old play house. Past all the childish things I used to do here.

I open the French doors that lead to the dining room and he follows me in, not bothering to close them. And then we're going up the stairs, his hand on my ass, pulling on my panties as we reach the second floor.

He pushes me against the wall, pressing his hard cock into my hips as he kisses my mouth. "We might not make it to the bedroom," he says.

"Oh, no, mister. You're not getting out of this house until you fuck me on my bed."

He laughs and starts tugging me down the hall, searching for my room.

But it's easy to find. There's a princess tiara painted on the door with my name underneath.

"Oh, fuck. You do not have a—" But then he pushes the door open and finishes his thought. "Yes, you do. You dirty little princess."

I do have a princess room. I'm talking a full-on mural of my own private kingdom, a knight on a white horse, and a rainbow on the ceiling.

"Fuck me," I say, walking over to the four-poster bed and turning around. "I wish you could tie me to this bed and show me what men really do with women in that position."

He looks at me like he might eat me up. Or eat me out.

I make it easy for him. I kick off my sandals, slip my panties down my legs, and push them aside with my toes. Then I climb onto the bed, my feet resting on the bedrails, and open my legs.

"Hungry?" I ask.

He walks towards me untucking his shirt.

We're going to fuck with clothes on, I already knew that. And he's right. It's sexy. Fucking with clothes on means you have limited time, you could get caught at any moment, or you can't be bothered to care.

Either way, when he unbuckles his belt and opens his pants to grab his hard, thick cock, wetness begins to pool between my legs.

He takes a few steps towards me, closing the distance, and then places his hands on my knees and opens my legs wider.

I stare down at his cock, resting just above my pink bedspread, and rearrange my skirt. Then I look up into his eyes and say, "First time in this bed."

He grabs my knees and jerks me forward so my ass is barely on the edge of the mattress, then grips my hips and slips his cock inside.

"Oh, God," I moan. I'm getting used to him, but it still hurts a little every time he enters me. "You're so big," I say. "So big. Too big for me."

"You're a dirty little thing," he says.

"Hey," I coo. "You're the one who wanted me to watch porn with you. All the girls say that and the guys love it. But here's a secret," I say, cupping my hand to my mouth. "You are too big, Ryker. You're so big I can feel you pressing up against my stomach when you—"

He thrusts inside me with a grunt. Gripping my hips so tight, I can feel them bruising.

"Yes," I moan. "Yes. Fuck me hard, and fast before we get caught. And this time," I say, "come inside me. I want you to fuck me hard on my bed and come inside me and—"

He pounds me. Hard. He's never taken me like this and I love it. I love it!

"Yes," I say. "Harder. Faster. Make me come before my parents get home."

He grabs my hair, seemingly out of control. But I'm not afraid. He's never out of control. He pushes me so my back bounces on the mattress, and then pounds me so hard, there's nothing but grunts and groans and the sound of his thighs slapping against mine.

"Come," he commands. "Come, right now!"

I do. I gush all over him. Squeezing his cock with my pussy until he stops, then lifts his head back and groans.

And that's when I feel it. That's how it feels. Because for the first time ever, he comes inside me.

I am in bliss. I am in heaven. I am complete and we are perfect together.

And then all of that fades away when I hear—

"Aria? Are you in here?"

—and realize my mother is coming up the steps and my bedroom door is wide open.

CHAPTER TWENTY

Is she up there? Aria's father calls. "Aria? Are you here? The back door was open."

"Maybe you should get the gun," her mother whispers.

Oh, shit.

I'd like to say there's enough time for me to get my pants up and look completely normal. Like I didn't just have sex with their daughter, in their house, in her princess bedroom, on her bed.

That doesn't happen. I get my dick tucked away and Ariel kicks her panties under the bed and straightens her dress. But if my hair looks anything like hers, this is nothing more than a futile attempt at innocence.

"Mr. North?" Mr. Amherst asks.

"Aria?" Mrs. Amherst asks.

"What exactly is going in here?" her father asks.

"Um…" we both say at the same time.

"Did you just… were you just…" He looks at me with an incredible expression of betrayal. That's the only way to describe the look on his face.

"Look," Aria says, "This is all new for us and—"

"New for you?" Amherst asks, looking at me, then at Aria. "This is the boy?"

"Boy?" I say.

Aria looks at me and frowns, then looks at her father and says, "Yes. This is the boy. We met that night of the board meeting and then again on my birthday. We've been dating a little ever since."

Amherst works his jaw a little. He's not a big guy. And he's in his fifties, so he's not going to punch me.

At least I didn't think he was. But he does. Right in the eye. "Get out of my house," he says, giving me a push towards the door. "Get out of my house and don't you ever come back here again, you sick son of a bitch! The deal is off. Do you hear me? The deal is off!"

"Daddy," Aria says. "Just listen, OK?"

"Get out!" Amherst says again, pointing at the door.

I glance at Aria's mother, who is silent and unreadable, then mutter, "Sorry," and walk out.

The whole time I'm walking down the path through the woods, Ozzy is texting me. *What the fuck happened? Where the fuck are you? Amherst called off the deal and said to ask you why.*

I ignore the texts, but he's waiting for me in front of the country club. "Dude," he says. "Do you know what's going on? Amherst is pissed. He fucking blocked my number! What the hell happened?"

Our car is waiting, so I just get in. Ozzy hesitates for a moment, like this can't possibly be happening but getting in this car will make it so. But then he realizes he has no choice and walks around to the other side and slides in next to me.

"You want to tell me how the fuck a deal we've been working on for over a month just suddenly disappears in one afternoon of country clubbing?"

"I'm dating his daughter," I say flatly.

"You're…" He laughs, then stops laughing abruptly. "No. No. No. Please tell me that the eighteen-year-old is not Aria Amherst."

"I wish I could. Well, that's a lie. I'm actually pretty infatuated with her." I look at my partner and best friend and I don't know what else to say except, "Sorry."

He huffs out an incredulous laugh. "You're sorry? You just blew up a two-hundred-million-dollar deal because you want to date a child and all you've got to say is *sorry*?"

"She's eighteen," I say. "She's not a child."

"Not only is she a child," Ozzy says, "she's the goddamned daughter of the man who was giving us the money to finish the project. Do you have any idea how fucked we are right now?"

"I have a pretty good idea," I say.

"Do you?" he asks. "You've been checked out for weeks and now I know why. You've been fucking her, haven't you?" He runs his fingers through his hair, messing it all up. "I can't believe you did this."

"I'll talk to him, OK? He's just... surprised right now. Aria and I will—"

"There is no Aria and you, Ryker. Not anymore. You're gonna give this guy the rest of the weekend to cool off and then on Monday you're going to pick up that phone, beg his forgiveness, tell him you'll never even look at his daughter again, and then hope to God he gives us this loan. That's what you're going to do."

"No," I say, shaking my head.

"No? No to which part? Because none of this is optional. No girl is worth two hundred million dollars."

"I'm not breaking up with her. If she wants to call it off with me, fine. I'll move on. But I'm not breaking up with her."

"You're going to throw away everything we've worked for over one girl who will maybe last another month, at most?"

"That's not what this is."

"Don't tell me." He laughs. "You're in love with her?"

I shrug and hold up my hands.

"Oh, for fuck's sake. I get it, OK? Mid-life crisis and all that. It sucks getting old. We all want to recapture our youth. But dude, you're blowing up your whole life over a girl who will use you to fulfill some older-man fantasy and then toss you aside the second a hot, buff, twenty-five-year-old comes along."

"Fuck you, Ozzy. You don't even know her."

"I don't need to know her. I've dated her. I've been where you are, Ryker. I've had my share of teenagers and believe me when I tell you, not only are they boring and stupid, they're not looking for a long-term thing with an older man unless they're poor and they need a sugar daddy. And Aria Amherst is the exact opposite of that. She has everything, why the fuck would she want you?"

I know he's right. I do understand this. Staying with me is a huge step down for Aria. She can only lose. But

211

I don't care. I look Ozzy straight in the eyes and say, "Then let her do that. But I'm not breaking up with her."

He stares at me for a few seconds. Then he shrugs and says, "Then I'm breaking up with you. Consider yourself bought out."

CHAPTER TWENTY-ONE

After Ryker walks out there's an awkward silence as my parents just stare at me in my bedroom.

"What did he do to you?" my father finally asks.

"He didn't do anything to me, Dad. We're dating!" I'm trying to be calm, but not really pulling it off. I just got caught having sex in my bedroom with a man almost twice my age.

"You are not dating!" my father roars. His face is all red with anger and he's breathing so hard I want to tell him to sit down before he has a stupid heart attack. "That man is a predator!"

"He is not. And we're in love!" I'm not really sure that's true. But we were definitely heading in that direction. "And this was all my idea, anyway. You can't blame Ryker for what just happened. I dragged him up here and—"

213

"I don't want to hear anymore," my father says, putting his hands up to his ears. "You're grounded, Aria. Until further notice. I trusted you in the city. Your mother and I both trusted you because you've always been the responsible one. The sweet one. The good one. And you betrayed our trust with... with... very bad decisions!"

"I didn't betray you," I say. I'm starting to get angry. "I like a man. That's all I did. I fell in love with a man. And I don't see what the big deal is." I look to my mother for help but she's frowning at me. "Mom," I say.

"Oh, no," my father says. "No. You're not going to play us against each other. You're grounded. From now on you will not leave this house except for school. I'll drop you off and pick you up—"

"You already do that, Dad."

"—and you won't set foot in the city without me by your side. And you can forget about any fun you had planned over summer, young lady! That's over."

"Plans?" I laugh. "I didn't have any plans. But you know what? I do now." I walk over to my closet and pull out my suitcase.

"Aria." My mother finally speaks up. "Put the suitcase away."

"No," I say. "I'm eighteen and I'm moving out."

"Honey," she says. "You haven't even graduated high school yet. You don't have anywhere to go."

"Don't I?" I ask. And now I've got attitude. I spent all my teenage years being this good little girl. This perfect role-model of a daughter. Never talking back, never drinking, never doing drugs, never having sex. And I'm tired of being that girl. I'm tired of being *sweet*.

"You cannot be thinking that Ryker North will let you stay with him?" My father laughs. But it's a bit hysterical. "He used you, Aria. And now that I've threatened to take away their loan, he will not even take your calls."

"We'll see about that," I say, still tossing things into my suitcase.

"I'll give them the loan," he says. "You stay here, promise to never see him again, and I'll give him the loan. You've ruined his business, Aria. Blown it all up. You have to know that. And if you stay here and be good, I'll put it all back together."

I hesitate inside my closet as I reach up and pull a shirt off a hanger. Thinking this offer through. Putting all the little pieces together in a logical way and decide... I'm sad.

I toss the shirt in my suitcase, then throw in a few pairs of jeans, one school uniform and some shoes, and close it up.

215

"You know what?" I say, turning to face my parents, then directing my words to my father specifically. "I've heard about bankers my whole life. How they ruined the world with bad loans, and how they take advantage of poor people while they collect fat bonuses and live in huge mansions that come with a country club. But I never believed you were one of them, Dad. I always thought you were one of the good ones. But this offer—" I shake my head. "I'm not blowing up Ryker's business plans. You are. And you're not doing it because he's not worthy, or because he can't pay back this loan, or because the project isn't a good idea. You're doing it because you don't like the thought of us dating. And I just want you to know… *that's* why I'm leaving."

And then I take off my grandmother's diamond ring, place it on my dresser, and walk out.

I had to wait on our front porch for an hour until the car I called finally arrived. By myself, because neither of my parents followed me out and I'm pretty sure they thought I was six and this was nothing but a childish bluff, but it wasn't.

That car came and I got in. And all the way into the city I prayed that my father didn't decide to remove his credit card from my ride app, because I had no money to pay for this ride if he did. And wouldn't that teach me a lesson? Running away using your daddy's credit card is the epitome of childish.

I don't call Ryker in the car because I'm not really sure how he's feeling right now and I don't want to give him a chance to tell me to go home. So when I arrive at his building—thank God the transaction goes through—I just walk inside, go up to the concierge, and tell them to announce me.

I fidget and worry as the woman at the desk calls up and tells Ryker I'm here. At least he's home. If he wasn't I'd have to take another car over to my sister's house and beg her to let me stay. And that's not something I want to do.

"He's coming down now, Miss Amherst," the concierge says, smiling at me.

"Oh," I say. "OK."

I don't know if that's good or bad. Will he turn me away? Tell me to go home so he can save his deal? I have a sick feeling in my stomach that I just made a huge mistake. What if he was just using me for sex? What if he chooses his business over me?

It would be the logical thing to do. Letting me up to his apartment means everything he's worked for goes up in flames.

I want to vomit, that's how stupid I feel right now. Why did I walk out on my parents? Why did I come all this way when I could've faced the facts in the privacy of my own home? Why did I ever think a man like Ryker could fall in love with me?

The elevator dings and Ryker steps out. He's frowning at me. "Aria, what's going on?" He looks around, like maybe my father is here too and this is some kind of intervention.

Then he spies my suitcase and his eyes meet mine.

"I'm sorry," I say. "I don't know what I was thinking. I shouldn't have—"

"Yes," he says, walking towards me to take my hand. "Yes."

And then he leads me into the elevator and we go up to his apartment.

When we step out he takes my suitcase and puts it aside. Then turns to me and pulls me into a hug. "I'm so sorry."

I hold him tight and sigh. "This is all my fault. It was a stupid idea to take you up to my bedroom. None of this would've happened if I had just acted more mature."

He chuckles, making a deep rumble noise in his chest. "Well… it's probably my fault for telling you about getting-caught sex that first time."

Which makes me smile and relax a little. But then I remember what my dad said in my bedroom after

Ryker left. "He really is going to cancel your loan," I say.

"I know. And Ozzy is probably going to buy me out."

I pull away from him and stare up into his eyes. "They why did you bring me up here?"

"Aria," he says, swiping my hair away from my face. "You are the most important thing in my life right now. I'm not going to give you up for money. Never. So just please, put that out of your mind."

"But you worked so hard for this," I say. "And now it's over."

"I worked hard for something," he agrees. "And money is nice, don't get me wrong. But there's lots of things money can't buy, and you're one of them."

I glance around and realize that I live here now. Maybe it's just a few days. Maybe it's longer, but tonight I will stay in his bed.

Another first.

Does he understand that?

"I thought you didn't want to play house with me?" I ask.

"What?"

"That's why I never stayed over. And now I'm staying over. So… we're playing house and you didn't want to do that."

"Oh, you sweet thing," he says, placing a hand on my cheek. "Listen to me, Aria. If you're ever in trouble and someone who claims to love you says they can't help you because of their principles, then they suck. They are not your friend. I don't give a shit about playing house. You're staying here with me where you'll be safe. I would never turn you away. Not in a million years."

I hug him again, feeling protected. "I think I love you right now."

"Yeah? Well, I think I fell in love with you that very first night we met. Come on," he says. "Let's get you unpacked and settled in."

He gives me a whole dresser even though I didn't bring enough clothes to fill it. And then he tells me we'll go shopping tomorrow and buy whatever I need. And on Monday he'll drop me off at school.

He smiles as he says that. But I just frown. "You don't feel weird about that?"

"That you're young, and still in high school, you mean?"

"Yes," I say. Pouting. Because I'm not as grown-up as I thought when I stomped out of my parents' house earlier trying to take a stand. I'm just a kid and he's an adult, and this will never, *ever* last.

Ryker looks at me thoughtfully, then takes my hand and pulls me over to the bed and pats the mattress. I sit. Wondering what he's gonna say.

"You have two weeks left of school. After four long years of high school you'll graduate and go to college. And four years later you'll wake up one day and realize you've now been out of high school longer than you were ever in it. And then four years after that you'll wake up and realize you've been out of college longer than you were ever in it. And one day, eighteen years from now, you'll wake up and realize you've been out of your parents' house longer than you were in it. This is just how life works. Time marches on and perspectives change. And hopefully, on the day after you turn thirty-six, you'll wake up and realize you've been with me longer than you've been without me."

I think about that for a second.

Then I put my arm around his waist and lean into his chest. "Thank you."

"I love you," he says. Then he picks up my hand and says, "Where's your birthday ring?"

"I gave it back," I say. "Because I don't want to be my daddy's girl anymore. I want to be yours."

CHAPTER TWENTY-TWO

First time coming inside her. First time making dinner together. First time sleeping in the same bed. First time making love in said bed. First time waking up, first time making breakfast… so many firsts happen in the span of twenty-four hours.

And then the first time dropping her off at school. Aria has mentioned her friends at school during our nightly conversations, but they are mostly just acquaintances. It's hard to forge true friendships outside of school when you live an hour away from everyone.

The cynical part of me wants to blame her father for that. Wants to think he might've done that on purpose to keep her at home on the weekends. Keep her distant from all her peers, both the ones in her neighborhood and the ones from school.

Because that's certainly how it turned out.

But I'm not that cynical when it comes to Mr. Amherst. I really do think he's just a guy who loves his family.

"I feel weird," Aria says, hand on the doorknob of my car as I idle in front of her school. When she put that uniform on this morning I wanted to bend her over and finger her pussy. Get her panties all wet and make her sit in school squirming and desperate because I left her hanging.

But I didn't. I might not have so much self-control tomorrow, but I held it together today. "About what?" I say.

"I dunno. Should I kiss you goodbye on the cheek like I do my father? Or climb in your lap and get you hard, then leave you hanging all day so you'll want to finger me in the car when you pick me up? Thanks for that, by the way. I appreciate the rides."

She is the sweetest fucking thing alive.

"You want me to choose? Because if you climb in my lap I'm going to pull around to the alley and give you a quickie before school."

She giggles and smiles. "Cheek then," she says, leaning over towards me. She places one hand on my far cheek and kisses the near one. Whispers, "I can't wait to go to bed with you tonight."

"I could stop by at lunch." I waggle my eyebrows at her.

"Oh, for sure. Do that. But I mean… just sleep next to you tonight. That's what I mean. Staying the night with you is the best thing ever." The school bell rings and she sighs. "I hope everything goes OK at work. I'm so sorry—"

"Don't apologize," I say. "Now scoot. You're going to get detention and then I'll have to spank you when we get home."

Her eyes open wide. "Hmmm."

"Out!" I say, pointing at the door.

She opens the door, laughing as she gets out and shuts it. Blowing me a kiss as she walks off.

I stare at her until she disappears inside the door, reluctant to go into work and face Ozzy, but knowing I have to do it.

The drive over is too quick. Everything is too quick. And before I know it I'm walking into the office and everyone is looking at me while simultaneously trying not to look at me.

Wonderful. He's already told the staff. I guess he's serious about this break-up thing.

"Ah," he calls from his office. "He shows."

I stop in his doorway, glancing over my shoulder, and find every single employee is watching us. "Should I come in and close the door?" I ask. "Or should we just hash this out in front of everyone since you've clearly already told them?"

Ozzy frowns at me. "I was angry."

"So?"

"So come in and close the door."

I do, then take a seat in the chair in front of his desk, casually propping an ankle on my knee like I've got all day.

"You took her to school, I take it? Mr. Amherst knows she's at your house. He checked her ride app and he's worried she's going to miss school."

"I did," I say. "Not that it's any of your business."

He shoots me an incredulous look. "You're joking, right? You just blew up the deal, Ryker. I should've known that drumming was a bad idea. I knew it would bring back memories, I just never thought you'd be that guy again. And I fucking told you to stay away from the young ones."

"So?" I say again. "Since when do I have to take your advice?"

"Since I pulled you out of that downward spiral you were on back in college and gave you something to work towards," he says.

"Work towards," I say, "is the key phrase there. Because I worked for all this."

"And you're about to throw it all away over a relationship that probably won't last through the weekend."

"You don't know that."

"Which part? The part where you get dumped by an eighteen-year-old girl once she realizes Daddy's not going to pay for her college? Or the part where you ruin the business we've spent the last ten years building? I get to have my say about this, Ryker. You're fucking me over, dude. Pretty goddamned hard, too."

"Look," I say, sighing heavily. "I like her. She likes me. Her father is freaking out over nothing. If it doesn't last, then hey, you all get your way. But if it does—"

"You're not listening to me, man! He pulled our loan! We're seventeen million dollars in debt. We can't finish our current projects unless we get his loan. Which means we can't sell them to pay back the fucking loans we already have. What the hell is wrong with you? You're thirty-five years old. You should've learned not to think with your dick by now."

"It's more than that," I say. "And frankly, I'm tired of explaining that to you."

"You're tired of explaining? I'm going to lose my penthouse. I'm going to lose everything over this girl, Ryker. Just..." He sighs. Gathers himself. Takes a deep breath and tries again. "Just tell her it's temporary. Just tell her you two have to break it off for a little while so we can get the loan and—"

"Lie to her father, then? That's your answer."

"It's not lying if you really do it."

"So I what? Kick her out and make her go home?"

"Yes!" Ozzy says. "Yes! Kick her out, make her go home. Apologize to her father—profusely—and then beg him to see this through as you promise never to touch her again."

I'm already shaking my head.

"Don't shake your head at me, asshole. We're going to lose everything! Do you really want to start over with nothing at thirty-five? Because I don't."

I know he's right. I get it. Losing this deal will ruin us. But selling Aria out for money is just so wrong. Even if we're lying to her father and we get back together. I don't want to do it. I want to keep her with me. I want her in my bed every night. I want to have lunch with her, and go grocery-shopping together, and have babies.

And more importantly, I don't want her father to hate me. I want him to bless this relationship and understand I'm going to take care of her the way she deserves.

"I don't want to," I say. "It's just as simple as that. I don't want to."

"Dude," Ozzy says, leaning back in his chair. "I do things I don't want to all the time. Do you think I wanted to take care of you when you got out of control? Do you think that was fun for me?"

I sigh again.

"It wasn't, OK? It sucked seeing you like that. But I showed up for you because you're like a brother to me. And if you can't show up for me for this, if you can't just put this girl on hold for a month or two so we can get these deals done, well... then I guess you're not the guy I thought you were."

We stare at each other for a few moments. Then he stands up, buttons his suit coat, and says, "I've got meetings today. Gonna placate nervous lenders and lie to them so they don't call our loans before the end of the day and make me fire all those people out there working their asses off for us."

And then he walks out.

Eventually I get up, go into my own office, and shut the door behind me. Sit at my desk and think about my options.

Aria or Ozzy.

Fucking wonderful.

Why does it always have to be this way? Why do people always have to choose?

I think about losing her. A month or two seems like a very short period of time. But I know what'll happen in those two months. Aria will graduate, probably go on some summer trip—courtesy of her parents. Backpacking through Europe or some shit. Just to get her away from me.

And they'll do that because they know it will work. They know she'll forget about me. She'll meet new people, and move on. And when she comes home for college in the fall, she'll be someone else.

She won't be my sweet thing ever again.

That's what I'm afraid of.

That this isn't real. That we're not in love. That there's nothing there but sex, even though I tried my hardest to keep that from happening.

And so it isn't fair, is it? To Ozzy, to her, to her family.

Keeping her for myself because I'm afraid she'll move on is no different than walking out on someone because you have a deal in the works.

My phone starts ringing soon after that. Business to do, people to talk to, shit to plan. And I do all that because it's my job.

But in the back of my mind I think about Aria and her parents.

And when three o'clock rolls around and it's time to pick her up from school, I know what the right thing to do is.

Take her home.

I have to take her home.

CHAPTER TWENTY-THREE

Well, Ryker doesn't show up at lunch for a quickie. But he left a message on my phone that he'll be there after school. I wasn't really expecting a quickie for lunch, but it was a good fantasy while sitting in calculus. In fact, I fantasized about him all day. I wrote my name out in cursive. Mrs. Aria North. Mrs. Ryker North. I did it over and over again. I pictured my wedding, and our honeymoon, and what our kids would look like.

The whole shebang.

And I loved every second of those fantasies.

I know how I got to his place is wrong. I understand that. My father is pulling his funding, his business partner is crazy upset, and my family life is a mess.

But I'm relieved that our relationship is now out in the open and we get to spend more time together.

It's not playing house, I tell myself. Yes, it's a little soon to move in together but everything about it feels right to me and I can't wait to see him after school.

He's waiting for me outside school at the curb with the parents. His silver sports car just a little bit out of place in the line of Mercedes and Audis the parents drive.

I didn't tell anyone what I did over break other than stay at my sister's and take the Photoshop class. No one was impressed. Not one word about the older man I'm now living with. Not one word about losing my virginity, or the game Ryker and I played in the Corinthian, or getting caught having sex in my bedroom.

No popular boys will be asking me to prom. In fact, I'm not going to prom. I was never going to have a date to begin with. I'm just not what these boys are looking for.

But that's OK. I'm what Ryker's looking for and that's all that matters now.

I wave at him as I open the car door and slide in. "Were you waiting long?" I ask, leaning over to kiss his cheek.

"No, not long," he says. He smiles at me, but then he frowns.

"Is something wrong? Did Ozzy yell at you today? Oh, God. Please tell me my father didn't show up at your work? He didn't text me all day. Not that he usually texts me, but you know. I didn't see him this morning and…" Ryker is just staring at me. "I'm rambling, sorry. What's up?"

"Aria," he says, taking my hand.

"What?" I ask, my heart starting to beat fast.

"You can't stay with me."

"What? Why not?"

"Just listen, OK? You're eighteen. You have high school graduation coming, and a whole summer before you start college in the fall—"

"So?" I say. Too loudly. "So what? I don't care about graduation. I don't care about any of it."

"That's my point. When we started this—when I started this—I didn't want to take over your life. I didn't want to change everything and rip it all apart."

"You're not!" I say. "You're not. I want this too, Ryker. I do."

"I know you do, Aria. I want it as well. But just… not like this."

"Not like what? What's changed? We were happy this morning."

"Yeah, and then I realized… well, I realized that taking you away from your family is the wrong way to start something real. You can't stay at my house. You have to go home. We have to sort this out and either your parents are on board, or we'll…"

"No," I say. "They don't get to make this decision, I do. We do," I say, taking both his hands. "I'm eighteen now. It's my life."

"I know," he says. "That's how I felt at eighteen."

"And you moved away. Everyone moves away. This is how things are done."

"Yeah, but you don't understand why I moved away, Aria. No one wants to leave the way I did, and if I take you now. If I let you move in and we seal the deal before we're ready—"

"We're ready," I say, becoming desperate.

But he shakes his head at me. Then he lets go of my hands, puts the car in gear and pulls away from my school. "We're not ready, Aria. We barely just got to know each other. Things are going too fast and I feel like we're skipping steps."

"Well, I don't feel like we're skipping steps."

He gives me a side-eyed look. "You don't actually know what the steps are."

"That was mean," I say.

"I'm not trying to be mean."

"Then what are you trying to do?"

He doesn't say anything for a few moments.

"Oh, my God. Are you breaking up with me?"

"No," he says, getting on the highway that leads to my parents' house.

"Well, you're taking me home."

"I'm not breaking up with you. Not exactly."

"Ryker," I say, starting to get pissed. "Explain. Tell me what the hell is going on."

"I just did, Aria. You're not listening to me. I'm taking you home and we're going to talk to your parents and see if they'll see things our way."

"And if not?" I ask.

"If not…" He sighs. "If not then we'll have to put this on hold."

"Is this about the deal?" I ask.

He points a finger at me. "Don't you dare. I'm doing this for you. For us. Not that deal or the money. So just don't even think that."

"I don't want to go home. Just take me to my sister's house then."

He looks at me, then back at the road. "Either we go to your house and have a conversation about this and respect your parents' wishes, or you break up with me. So which way does this go, Aria? It's up to you."

"You're serious?"

"Dead serious."

I lean back in my seat and cross my arms, so pissed off. "Why do you get to make all these decisions? Why don't I get a say?"

"You do get a say. You either do it my way and give us a real chance to make this work or you break it off with me. Because those are my terms."

"Those aren't terms!" I shout. "That's an ultimatum!"

"You can think of it that way if you want. But that's not how I see it."

"What if I give you an ultimatum?"

"That's your prerogative."

"Nice," I huff. "Real nice."

He sighs, then takes my hand again. "Just... give me a chance to make it right, OK? Just trust me, Aria. If I ruin your relationship with your family you will resent me for as long as we're together. It might not happen right away, but it will happen. And I can't live with myself if I do that."

I pull my hand away from his, so angry right now. I feel like I did that day back in the Corinthian hotel restaurant when he ordered me grilled cheese. Like a stupid child.

I take deep breaths as we drive, trying my best not to sigh on the exhale and huff and puff like I'm having my own silent tantrum.

But I am having my own silent tantrum. Which makes me feel even worse. Because he's right and I know he's right, I'm just scared that this will be the last time I ever see him and all those fantasies I had today will end up being just that. Fantasies.

My parents are never going to be OK with this. Never. I can't imagine a single explanation that might sway them over to our side and make them happy at the same time.

And I don't even blame them for that. I just... want what I want.

Before I know it, we're pulling into my driveway. My father's car is there, which I was not expecting since he usually stays at work until at least five. And that means he didn't go into work today. He stayed home because he was upset with me.

Ryker turns the car off and takes my hand again. "Ready?"

"Does it matter if I'm ready?"

"Of course it does, Aria. All your feelings matter."

"You just get to make the final decision though, right?"

"If you want to see it that way, I can't stop you. But I promise," he says, squeezing my hand. "That's not what's happening."

I pout and frown.

"Just trust me."

He gets out of the car but I don't. I sit, refusing to budge. But he just walks around to my side, opens my door, and offers me his hand.

I take it. Reluctantly. And get out of the car.

He holds my hand all the way up the walk to the porch and even though I have never in my life knocked on this door, I feel like I should knock.

I even raise my knuckles to do that, but Ryker pushes my hand down and says, "You live here, Aria. This is your home."

So I open the door and walk inside. My parents are both standing at the bottom of the stairs like they were waiting for us.

"I called them ahead of time," Ryker says. Then he lets go of my hand and says, "Please," as he motions to the front living room, like he wants us all to go in there for a chat. "I'll only take a minute of your time."

We all go in to the living room, my mother coming to my side to pull me into a sideways hug and give me a squeeze, my father frowning at everyone, like he's not in the mood for talking and wants Ryker out of here as quick as possible.

But Ryker takes a seat on the couch and leans back. Hands on his knees. "I know this isn't what you want for Aria."

I open my mouth to protest that they don't get to decide that anymore, but Ryker puts up a hand and says, "Please, Aria. Let me speak and then you can have your say."

"Fine," I say. But I pull away from my mother and take a seat next to Ryker. I want them all to know what my decision is. Even if none of them care.

"I'm not going to take your daughter away from you, Mr. Amherst. And I already told her that we can't date unless we have your permission."

My father is already shaking his head, already opening his mouth to say something, but before he can, my mother speaks. "Harold," she says. "You were almost fifteen years older than me when I got pregnant with April at eighteen. And we had to face my parents and your parents in less than ideal conditions as well. So you will shut your mouth and let this man have his say, so help me God, or you will leave the room. He came all the way out here, brought our daughter home, and now we're going to hear him out. Do you understand me?"

241

Holy shit. My mom just put her foot down. I have never seen them fight before. Not that she's even raising her voice, because she is the epitome of grace and manners right now. But they have always presented themselves as a unified front and any and all discussions where they were at odds always took place behind closed doors, so I've never seen this side to her.

"Doris," my father protests.

But she puts up her hand to silence him. "No. Let Mr. North speak." Then she looks at Ryker and says, "Go ahead, Mr. North. You were saying?"

She winks at me. I blink at her in surprise.

But there's no time to process that wink because Ryker takes a deep breath and begins speaking again.

CHAPTER TWENTY-FOUR

"*I came from a pretty messed-up* situation at home," I begin. "My father left when I was four and never sent my mother a dime to help out."

"Oh, I'm so sorry," Doris says. "That must've been difficult."

"It was and it wasn't," I say. "My mother and I grew very close in those early years. Like we were a team, ya know? A real family, just the two of us. Just her and me for almost ten years because her parents got divorced early and didn't pay much attention to her, or me, for that matter. But then she met this man and I didn't like him. To be honest, there wasn't much to like about him. He treated my mother like crap and me even worse. But she was tired. Tired of raising me alone. Tired of working two, sometimes three jobs just to stay afloat. Tired of just existing. So maybe he wasn't her Prince Charming? She often told me she loved my father, even after he left. So Prince Charming didn't get her anywhere."

Aria takes my hand and gives it a squeeze when I pause for too long.

"And when I was about to graduate high school my stepfather said we were moving away from Kentucky to Nebraska where he could find work. He was in the natural gas business and the industry was dying in Kentucky. But I didn't want to go, so I said that. And he said I wasn't invited. That it was time for me to pull my weight, like he did when he was my age, and find a job and be on my own."

"That's terrible," Doris says.

"I didn't realize it was terrible at first. Because I figured my mom would stay with me. But she didn't," I say. Aria squeezes my hand again. "She left with him."

"She left you?" Aria says.

I nod. "She did. And she never looked back. And I felt kinda betrayed, ya know?"

"Of course you did," Doris says. "That's… I just can't imagine doing that to one of my children."

"No," I say, looking at Aria. "No, you guys would never do that to each other." I look at her father. "The Amhersts are a family," I say. "A very tight one too. And when I met Aria I had no intention of breaking you apart." I turn a little to face Aria. "I can't take this away from you, Aria. Even if you think I'm the greatest guy in the world. Because it's no fun when your family turns their back on you. And if you stayed with me, sure, I could take care of you. Even if your father didn't want to pay for your college next year, I could do that. I would do that if it came down to it. But it's not going to come down to that. I won't allow it. This is your family and it's a good one. If having you right now means I come between all this, then I can't have you."

"Ryker," she says.

"Just wait," I say. "And listen. Because if you stay with me without the blessing of your parents then I'm that guy, ya know? The one who comes in mid-stream and rips everything apart. And you'd be the one walking out, Aria. Not them. And I won't let you make that mistake. Because after my mom left I got into all sorts of bad things. Drugs, drinking, sex," I say, glancing up at her father, then avert my eyes. "I was in a garage band and did things wannabe garage band members do when they have no real future. But I had worked hard in my first few years of high school trying to make my mother's new boyfriend like me and I had a scholarship waiting for me here. So I came here, worked three, sometimes four jobs to pay for that first year, but I wasn't doing great. I was still on drugs, still messing up, and I was about to be kicked out of school when I met Ozzy. Mr. Herrington," I clarify for her parents.

"Ozzy straightened me out. He helped me get through the next year. Gave me a loan, which I paid back," I say, looking at Mr. Amherst. "My word is good. I promise you, it is. Or Ozzy Herrington wouldn't be partners with me. So I'm here to give you my word. If you could just… give us a chance—that's it. That's all

I want. Just give Aria and me a chance to see if this is real or not—I'd appreciate it. Because even though I don't know your daughter the way you do, I'm falling in love with her. I know she's the right girl for me because she's sweet, and kind, and honest, and smart. And she's all those things because you made her that way. But if you say no, then I'll respect that. I give you my word, I will respect your wishes. Because I want you too," I say. "I want all of you. I don't just want her."

I pause as they all look at me, then throw up my hands and say, "That's it. That's my big speech."

Doris looks at her husband, who sighs. Then she says, "Will you two excuse us for a minute so we can have a discussion?"

"Sure," I say.

Aria turns to me and says, "I'm sorry. I had no idea."

I sigh, feeling relieved to get all that off my chest. "I don't want you to go through what I did when my mom left. And I don't want your parents to go through that either, Aria. So whatever they decide, we'll respect it. And if they say no, we'll take a long break and maybe we can have lunch sometime in the fall and see where we're at."

"The *fall*?" She pouts.

"I told you I wanted to do this right and I meant it. If we're really in love now we'll still be in love then."

246

She leans her shoulder into mine and sighs. "OK," she says. "That's fair."

We sit like that for a good twenty minutes before her parents return. Mr. Amherst takes a seat in a chair while Doris sits on the other side of Aria.

Amherst clears his throat, then says, "OK."

"OK?" Aria asks. "What's that mean?"

"It means I have conditions," he continues. "First, Aria lives here." He points to the floor. "At home."

"Done," I say.

"Second, you do not pick her up from school. That's my job. And you do not see her during the school week."

"Done," I say.

"Third…" He sighs.

"Go on," Doris says. "Finish it."

"Third," he repeats. "You have lunch with us every Sunday in the city. And that's the only day you two get to see each other until the summer is over."

"Dad!" Aria protests.

"Done," I say.

"Ryker," she says, turning her frustrations to me.

247

"It's all good, Aria. One day a week is a very good start to a new relationship."

"No," Aria says, standing up. "I get to negotiate too. I'm capable of making my own decisions."

"I told you," her mother says.

Her father looks at her and nods. "OK, Aria. Renegotiate then."

"One," Aria says, pacing the floor in front of the couch. "I live here but Ryker can come visit any time he wants."

Amherst glares at me, but he nods. "Done."

"Two," Aria says. "He can pick me up from school on Fridays. There's only two left anyway. And," she continues, "we get to have a date that night with no curfew."

Her father hesitates so long on this one, her mother intercedes. "Done," Doris says.

Aria smiles, feeling brave. "And three... we can see each other two days a week all summer long. And then all the restrictions are over. I'll be in college and I can make up my own mind about who I chose to date."

Her father lowers his head and for a moment I think he's angry. But then I catch him smiling.

He knew. He knew Aria would put up a fight. He was expecting this. Maybe it was a test, not just for me, but for both of us. A test to see if I respected him enough to give in and if she was grown-up enough to fight for what she wanted.

"You drive a hard bargain, Aria," her father says, hiding his smile before he looks up. "But you're going to make an excellent businesswoman one day. Done."

Doris makes a big production of sighing, then she sniffles a little as she wipes her eyes and says, "Would you like to stay for dinner, Ryker?"

And I reply, "I can't think of a single other place I'd rather be."

CHAPTER TWENTY-FIVE

I learned a lot about myself during that negotiation with my mom and dad. I learned that family matters even though they sometimes make you want to stomp your feet and pull your hair out. I learned that Ryker has a past. A childhood. A mother. A friend who was there for him.

Which I hadn't thought about before that moment, but it gave weight to his argument that we needed to take this slow. New relationships can destroy old ones if we're not careful.

And sometimes that can be bad or it can be good.

Ryker's mom gave up Ryker for a man. That's what I was about to do with my family before Ryker told his story and made me really think this through. My family didn't do anything to deserve a severing of ties. So I'm glad Ryker told me about his experience so I didn't have to make the same mistake his mother did.

But letting go of old relationships and forging new ones can be good sometimes too. Ryker let go of his mother and found Ozzy. Sometimes it's necessary to move on, sometimes it's necessary to cling to the past.

It's hard to know which is which, so having people you trust—people who love and support you and give you good advice—well, that's something money can't buy. It has to be earned.

There's a lot more to this grown-up stuff than having sex, and moving out, and getting your own car. You need to be careful with people you love and not take those feelings for granted.

I did get a car. My parents bought me one for graduation today. And the moment I saw it sitting in our driveway with a giant red bow on the roof I understood why I got the ring for my birthday.

The ring was a symbol of our family ties. My parents wanted me to know that yes, I'm an adult now, but they will always be here for me.

The car is a symbol of freedom.

Which is great when you know freedom doesn't really have anything to do with driving away and there is always a home base to come back to.

Ryker and I are sitting in his car driving to his place. Graduation is over, the celebratory dinner with my family is over, and now we're on our way to his place for our Friday night date.

"Do you feel any different?" he asks me, pulling up to the valet of his building.

I smile at him, getting lost in his eyes for a moment. "Not yet," I say. "But the night's not over."

Then the doorman is opening my door and I get out. Ryker joins me, taking my hand as we walk into the building together.

"Oh, Miss Amherst," the concierge calls from the desk. "Your package came." She lifts a shopping bag out from behind the counter and walks it over to me.

"What's this?" Ryker asks, as I take the bag and tip her.

"Thank you so much," I tell the concierge. Then to Ryker I say, "You'll see." I smile at him and urge him towards the elevator.

He grins at me all the way up to his penthouse. "What are you up to?" he asks, just as the elevator doors open.

But I just wink at him and enter the apartment.

"Aria?" he prods.

I turn and hold the bag out for him. "I have a gift for you."

"For me?" He chuckles. "It's your graduation night and I didn't even give you your gift yet."

"Oh, believe me, this is a selfish gift. I'm getting something out of it too. Open it," I say, placing the bag on the coffee table.

His grin is wide and his eyes are bright. I hope he guesses. I hope he's surprised. I hope for everything.

Inside the bag is one shiny black shirt box with a thick, pink, satin ribbon. "Hmmm," Ryker hums, still beaming as he pulls on the ribbon and it dissolves instantly into a luxurious pile of softness.

He lifts the lid off the box and just chuckles as he holds up the black lace corset. "What's this?" he asks.

"Surprise," I say.

Then he looks down into the box and says, "What, no panties?"

I just laugh and say, "Open the other box and you'll see why."

Because there is another box inside. A small one, just like the first. One that might hold a key fob or maybe a new wallet.

That's not what's inside.

"Oh, Aria." He chuckles, holding up the stainless-steel butt plug with a pink, heart-shaped jewel handle.

"We've been dabbling with them for weeks now and I think I'm ready for the real thing. So this is how it's going to go tonight, Mr. North. I'm going to put that corset on and then you're going to put that plug in my ass and fuck my pussy. Then you're going to take it out and give me the real thing. Because I want to be more than your sweet thing. I want to be your naughty thing too."

He side-eyes me, still grinning like a wild man.

But before he can say anything I step towards him and place two fingers on his lips. "Yes," I say. "I'm sure. Now help me out of these clothes."

He leans down to kiss me first. It's a long, soft, open-mouthed kiss that gets all my sweet parts tingling. And as he does that he unzips my dress and slowly drags it down my shoulders until it drops to the floor at my feet.

He stands back, his gaze moving up and down my body. Taking in my choice of underwear. "Black and pink, huh?"

"Sweet with a side of naughty," I say. "Just the way we like it."

His grin turns serious and hungry as he pops the clasp between my breasts and removes my bra. Then eases

255

my panties down my legs, bending as he lowers them, so he can kiss my stomach as I step out.

His hands go to my hips, gripping them with just enough pressure to let me know what he thinks of my gift tonight, then he slides them down my thighs, my knees, my calves and takes off my heels.

When I'm standing naked and bare in front of him, he looks up at me, both hands reaching up to my breasts, and squeezes them as he inhales.

The wetness pools between my legs with anticipation and he stands up again, reaching for the corset.

He puts it on me slowly, carefully. The way he's done everything with me since we started over. Hooking up the back with concentrated deliberateness. I peek over my shoulder when he's done and see him reaching for the butt plug. He holds it in his hand for a moment, the stainless steel and gemstone handle glinting in the light.

Then he says, "Come over here, Aria," as he takes my hand and leads me over to the sitting area. "Bend over and place your hands here," he says, motioning to the back of the couch.

I do, stretching my back so I can reach, while opening my legs so I can be sexy.

"That's nice," he says. "Very, very nice."

He walks away for a moment, going into the bedroom. I glance over my shoulder when he returns holding a tube of lubricant.

He squeezes some out and rubs it all over the butt plug, then says in a low, deep voice that I now recognize as desire, "Relax, while I play."

I suck in a deep, deep breath. Knowing this plug is bigger than the others we've used so far. A little bit apprehensive but mostly just curious what having him inside me will feel like. Ryker takes his time. Using his fingers first. Sometimes playing with my pussy and rubbing my clit to keep me excited.

There's no chance of me becoming *unexcited*.

I dreamed about this last night. Woke up wet and horny. Sat through graduation and dinner with my parents still fantasizing about it. We've watched porn together a few times and I like the ones where the man enters her ass as they lie side by side, then pulls her on top of him. I don't know why that position excites me so much. Maybe because the guy usually reaches around to stroke her pussy as he fucks her. Maybe because her legs are open and she's exposed because the guy is underneath her.

I'm not sure, but I hope we try that position today.

"Are you ready?" Ryker asks, rubbing his hand up and down the cheek of my ass.

I nod, then say, "Yes."

257

He begins by rocking the butt plug back and forth into my asshole. "Relax," he says, as he steps to the side a little and begins caressing my breast. They are full and hanging down, my nipples peaked and tight. He pushes the plug into the firm muscles, finding resistance, but I exhale and close my eyes and the tip enters me.

It's thicker than the other plug and I can feel the difference immediately. But it's not nearly as wide as Ryker's cock. There's a moment of pain and doubts creep in. Like maybe this is a mistake and maybe we should do this another time.

But then it's all the way in and I remember why I asked for this to begin with.

"I love that," I say.

He takes a step back and caresses my ass cheeks with both hands, then says. "It's beautiful, Aria. You're beautiful. Do you want to see what you look like? How I see you right now?"

I bite my lip and nod. "Yes."

A few seconds later he snaps a pic with his phone and then sits down on the couch beside me, sinking into the couch cushions. "Look," he says, holding up the phone.

I don't move. I stay just as he wants me. But I turn my head a little to see the image.

My legs are open and I'm bent over enough so the lips of my pussy are clearly visible. And just above them is the diamond-shaped jeweled handle pressed flat up against my asshole.

I look away and up at Ryker. Find him smiling. "I look pretty sexy," I say.

"You're so sexy, I want to fuck you in the ass right now."

"Will you?" I ask.

He shakes his head. "No, not yet. I want you to suck my cock, Aria. Get down your knees, take it out, and put it as deep inside your mouth as you can."

He hasn't let me do that yet. All my blow jobs so far have come with restrictions. *Just the tip, Aria. Just the head, Aria. Just lick my shaft, Aria.* Never has he let me take him any farther than that.

I do as he requests. Get down on my knees and pull his shirt out of his pants and start unbuttoning it. I have to lean forward to get the top buttons so I use that opportunity to kiss him on the mouth. He grins and kisses me back. But he takes my hands and returns them to the buckle on his belt.

My forearm is resting on his upper leg, over the top of his long, thick cock. He's not wearing underwear today and it's so long it stretches down the length of his thigh.

His belt buckle jingles as I undo it. Then I pop the button of his slacks, pull his zipper down, and reach inside to grab his cock. He hisses, and I watch his face as I take him out and hold him in my fist.

I lean down with my mouth open and put his entire swollen head inside my mouth. His hand immediately goes to my head, twisting my long hair in his fingertips as he urges me to go down on him. I gag a little, but breathe through my nose as I open my mouth as wide as I possibly can and then part of his shaft is inside me and I feel the warm, tingling wetness between my legs as I take him just a little bit more.

He repositions his body. Sliding his hips down towards the edge of the couch so he can see me better. We lock eyes and both of us smile.

He takes another picture with his phone and holds it up.

His cock is so fat, my mouth open so wide.

We're doing dirty, smutty stuff but I feel beautiful when I see that picture. I see what he sees and I like it.

"Bob your head a little," Ryker says. "Try fucking me with your mouth. Just a little," he encourages. "Just give me a taste."

A taste. I think about that for a moment. As in a sample of what's to come.

I lean down, gagging again. Then pull back as I seal my lips around his shaft to have more contact with him.

"Oh, yes," he says. "That's very nice. Do it again." And when he says that, he presses a button on his phone and I hear the tell-tale chime of a video beginning to record.

I do it again. And again. And again. My eyes on his every time. Then I close them and go down, holding his cock deep in my mouth as I hold that position until I think I might choke, and have to pull back.

He stops the video and turns it around, playing it back for me so I can see what he sees.

I smile around the head of his cock.

"OK," he says. "I can't wait any longer. Help me take off my clothes, starting with my cufflinks."

I let his cock fall out of my mouth, dripping with saliva, and reach for his cuff, my fingers popping the cufflink off and placing it in his hand. I repeat this for the other cuff, and then he sets the links aside on the end table.

I love taking off his shirt. I love seeing his tattoos appear on his arms. I love how he goes from serious businessman to tatted-up bad boy when I drag his sleeves down his arms. I love how muscular he is. How hard his arms are. How small and protected I feel when he's got them wrapped around me.

"Now the pants," he says.

261

I reach for his waist and tug them down. He lifts up his hips to help me as I drag them down his legs and leave them on, just below his knees.

"I want to fuck you with pants on, Mr. North."

He smiles wide. "That's sexy," he says. "In case you didn't know."

"Someone told me that once," I quip, climbing up into his lap. The butt plug feels intense. A little painful, but in a good way. He's fucked me with one in before, so I know the sensations will only intensify as we move forward, but how much? I'm not sure. The only thing I'm sure about is that I want to experience this with him.

I balance myself on my knees, hovering over his thighs. His cock is wet and glistening from my mouth as I wrap my fingers around it and place it at the entrance of my pussy. This makes me recall that first time. When he put me in charge of my experience. How he told me to go as fast or as slow as I wanted.

Now I'm more experienced, more comfortable with my erotic side—so I don't take my time like I did back then. I linger a little when the head of his cock is fully inside me, but only because I want to fully experience the sensations. And then I drop myself on top of him. Fully appreciating how he stretches me and fills me up and how the pressure from the larger butt plug intensifies all the feelings.

Ryker places his hands on my cheeks, then his fingertips thread up into my hair.

It's not going to take me long. I already know I'm close to coming. But I want to hold off as long as I can. So once he's fully inside me I pause to take Ryker in. Place my hands on his cheeks too.

"I love you," he says. "I know it's early and that saying those words might scare you, or put you off, or—"

"I love you too," I say, trying to ease any insecurities he has about saying those words.

He just smiles at me as I begin to move. Rising up and sitting down. My hands on his shoulders now, because I love the way my palms cup so perfectly around the curve of muscles. And how they move when he places his hands on my hips and starts to encourage me.

Then one sneaks over to my belly and his thumb dips down to play with my clit.

This is the part I like best. When he's in me, and we're using the plug, and he flicks the pad of his thumb over that sweet spot.

It drives me wild.

"Yes," I moan.

"Yes," he growls back.

Instead of me lifting up and sitting down, he begins to rock me back and forth across his lap and the climax begins to build. The tingly, warm sensations course through my body.

"Come, Aria," he hums. "Come for me and I'll reward you with another first."

I love our firsts but even if I wasn't eager to experience that, there's no way I can't come.

It's different this time. Different than all the other times. Because we're having another first tonight. One I hadn't thought about.

First time making love instead of having sex.

It's not an explosion. It's a slow, pulsating, life-altering, mind-bending experience that makes me feel like I just touched his soul.

It's lovemaking.

I lean over, placing my head on his shoulder so my mouth is right against his neck. And I kiss him as I enjoy the contractions that come in the wake of the release. He gives me this time afterward. Always wants me to come at least once before we move to the more explosive, hard sex.

But I don't want to wait. So I sit up and swing my leg over, glancing down at his hard cock, and see my come glistening on his shaft. "How do you want me?" I ask him.

"Jesus," he says, staring up at my eyes. Then he says, "Exactly how I placed you before."

I smile and nod. Positioning myself leaning over with legs spread and hands on the back of the couch as he stands up, kicking off his shoes and taking off the rest of his clothes.

Then he puts one hand on my hip and begins to tug on the crystal handle of the plug. Turning it inside me as he slowly pulls it out.

He drops it on the floor with a loud clunk, and then spreads my ass cheeks with both hands and leans down to kiss me on the small of my back.

The sensation of his heavy breathing and soft kiss tickle me a little so I shudder and arch my back. "Don't make me wait," I say. "Don't make me beg."

And as soon as those words leave my mouth he's pressing his cock up to my asshole. There is almost no resistance. No pain because the plug has me totally relaxed. And then he's inside me.

Fully inside me in a way I've never experienced before. My ass tightens in response.

"Aria," he moans. "You're killing me."

"Fuck me," I say. "I want to feel it. I need to feel it."

He pushes in, just a little, and I close my eyes and hang my head. It feels so good.

265

Then he pulls back and pushes forward again. Then again, and again, and pretty soon he's fucking me harder and harder. His thighs slapping up against my ass. And then I feel something new.

Oh, God, I don't know what it is. Something hitting my clit—and then I realize it's his balls swinging between my legs and crashing against my pussy.

I didn't plan on coming again so quick, I just can't help it. I squeeze him as the climax floods my body and he moans, "Yes, yes, yes. Clamp down on my cock, Aria."

I couldn't stop that if I wanted to.

He slows again, letting me enjoy the aftershocks of pleasure. Then he says, "Don't let me pull out. I'm going to sit on the couch."

That excites me and I do as I'm told. Moving slowly, carefully, so as not to break our connection. And a few seconds later I'm sitting. In his lap again, only this time we're not facing each other.

He pulls me into his chest, protective arms tight around my middle, just under my breasts, and he says, "Now slowly open your legs."

I do, and just that simple move makes me want to come again. Because my pussy feels so exposed.

He hands me his phone and whispers, "Take a picture for me, Aria. I want to see you like this. I want to see *us* like this."

I take the camera and point it at me, making sure it's angled right to get my sweet pussy in the frame, and press the screen before handing it back.

"Oh, fuck," he moans into my neck. "I need you to come quick now, sweet thing. Because I don't know how long I can last."

His fingers reach around to my belly and slowly drop to my clit where they begin to strum. Back and forth, slow at first, then faster and faster and I find myself out of control. Moaning, and wailing, and screaming, and yes, coming. Again.

I'm not even done when he stands up, disconnecting us, and spins me around on the floor so I'm on my knees in front of him. Legs open, eyes up. He pumps his cock hard a few times, grimacing and moaning.

Then I nod to Ryker. I give him permission to do what he's fantasizing about.

He aims the head of his cock at my mouth and I open wide just as his hot, sweet semen bursts out in pulsating waves on my tongue.

I never take my eyes off him.

I never want to take my eyes off him again.

Aria's father didn't cancel the loan. In fact, that whole project was a huge success. We have now officially sold two commercial buildings and seven refurbished houses. And twenty of the local residents have taken us up on the special refinance loans to rehab their homes. The Gingerbread neighborhood is getting a facelift.

Ozzy didn't break up with me. Our partnership is now stronger than ever and he's even come over for Sunday lunch with the Amhersts a few times. I think he's got his eye on April, who may or may not be playing hard to get.

And the pinnacle of our investment came to fruition for the Fourth of July festival. I did get my friend Kenner to meet April, and while she was super excited and impressed, the really cool part is that Kenner got his band to agree to play a song for the neighborhood as a surprise.

Thousands of people showed up out of nowhere once the word got out that Son of a Jack was playing. By the end of the day every food vendor had sold out, every home that was for sale had half a dozen showings lined up, and the local news even came and interviewed Ozzy and me on TV.

Aria stood by my side the whole time. And when the local reporter asked who she was, I said, "This is Miss Aria Amherst. My girlfriend."

Which got an eyebrow lift from more than a few people until Mr. Amherst came over to introduce himself.

He likes me. I can tell. And so does her mother. But I did everything right to make that happen.

Do I enjoy only seeing Aria twice a week?

Yes, actually. I do. By the time the weekend rolls around I'm dying for her.

Dying for her.

She is everything I've ever wanted.

Young and pretty, sure.

Sweet and dirty, yes.

But most of all she's just… mine.

I have plans for us. So many plans for us. They include things like brand-new diamond rings. A wedding, a honeymoon, and of course, children.

But Aria has plans for us too.

Living separately and dating while she's in her first year of college. And fixing up the old Victorian house we bought down the street from April's apartment.

She's worth the wait. And it's not a hard wait. It's bliss. She is everything I've ever wanted in a woman and her family is the perfect package deal.

She is, and will always be, my sweet thing.

But one day, eighteen years from now, I know we'll wake up and realize...

We've been together now longer than we were ever apart.

And if that's not a happily ever after, I don't know what is.

Welcome to the End of Book Shit where Julie gets to blab about anything she wants. If you're new to the EOBS (as we like to call it) then there's two things you need to know about it. One – it's never edited. I write these after the edits and proofs are finished. So you have to forget about all the fucks you give about typos when you read it. Second—I do have a tendency to ramble so sometimes they totally pertain to the book or the process and sometimes they don't. Also, I like to swear and generally just say anything I want. So if you're offended at the end, I don't apologize for that.

So back in 2015 I wrote a little book called EIGHTEEN. It was a semi-autobiographical story

273

about my life when I turned eighteen. And let me tell you, my life was pretty messy back then. It made a great backbone for a story though. Not all of it is real. I made some stuff up. Hardly anyone has a life so interesting they don't need to fictionalize certain aspects of it in a "memoir" type book. Not even me. ;)

But the whole point of the book was in the tag line. Which was: Eighteen is hard. Because for me, it was. Super confusing, and stressful, and so many things going on. So many new choices to make and so many new decisions to live with.

And when I first came up with this trio of books (Pretty Thing, Sweet Thing, and the last one is Wild Thing) I didn't want them to be a series. And they're not. Once Wild Thing releases they will be grouped into a series called Naughty Things, but they aren't grouped together because there's crossover in the world or the characters. Just in the tropes.

Pretty Thing is brother's best friend, Sweet Thing is young girl-older man, and Wild Thing is captive submissive. You're probably thinking… hmmm. Those don't really go together. And you're kinda right. They are all very different with one exception.

They are all a "little bit taboo". Not a lot. None of them are terribly dark for one thing and that's what most people think of when they hear the word taboo.

But they are a little. Just a little bit taboo.

Anyway, it's not all that important except that's how I came up with the idea for Sweet Thing. And the real main point is that I didn't think about my book Eighteen until way after I started writing Sweet Thing. Maybe even when I was finally writing the end.

And that's when it hit me that I was really writing Eighteen from another perspective.

Eighteen, the book, is about a girl with no family ties, no support system, and no one to fall back on except this hot older man who kinda takes over her life. And Pretty Thing is the total opposite.

Unlike Shannon (my alter-ego in Eighteen), Aria has everything when she turns 18. She's rich, she lives in a huge mansion in the suburbs but commutes into the city for private school, she has a mom and a dad who give a shit, and a sister she doesn't hate.

I might even go so far as to say Aria is the "Me" I wish I was back then. I've written about my secret teenage life as a horse-crazy girl and how by day I used to hang out with the cool kids at school and at night I worked at this show jumping barn to pay for riding lessons. And at the time this show jumping barn was like the best. So all the rich kids from Cleveland used to commute out to this barn three or four times a week to take their lessons. And they all boarded their super-expensive pedigree jumpers out there too. I was the girl who took care of the horses and tacked them up before lessons. And I guess I always knew that I was different from these kids. I lived close by in these middle-class suburbs, I went to public school, and I lived in an apartment with my single mother. But that's just the kind of neighborhood I lived in. *My* life was normal. These super rich kids at the barn, that was the abnormal life from my perspective.

I knew we were different deep down. But it never really meant anything to me until one summer I was working at the barn every day. And one of these rich girls invited me over to her house to hang out.

And I remember walking in to her house thinking… God, this is nice. And I didn't live in a shitty apartment, OK? My home was nice. My mom was in to nice things. But it was an apartment. I had never lived in a house as a kid. So I remember thinking… I wish I was this girl. What is her life like? How is my life different?

Well, you only have to read Eighteen to know what my life was like.

So when I finished up Sweet Thing all this stuff hit me. Aria is that girl I wish I was when I turned 18. I might even go so far as to say Aria is "Shannon" (from Eighteen) if Shannon had a father who gave enough shits to stick around.

I hardly ever wish I was someone else. I sometimes wish I was different. Taller, for sure. Maybe even nicer. lol Because I'm not one of those outgoing people at all. But even though my life has had lots of hard times I don't want to take any of it back. I don't want to miss out on the lessons I learned or learn them some other way.

But I quite enjoyed imagining Aria's life when I was writing this book. Also, I really loved that Ryker was so totally different than Mateo in Eighteen. He was older, he was richer, but most of all, he was a lot more careful with Aria than Mateo was with Shannon. I think I respect Ryker more than I do Mateo. Mateo was a bulldozer. He wanted to force Shannon to see things a new way. And Ryker was more of a gentle guiding hand.

So no huge dark twists in this story. It's just… sweet.

That was the whole point.

Thank you for reading, thank you for reviewing, and I'll see you in the next book (which is WILD THING!!)

Julie
JA Huss
April 13, 2019

JA Huss never wanted to be a writer and she still dreams of that elusive career as an astronaut. She originally went to school to become an equine veterinarian but soon figured out they keep horrible hours and decided to go to grad school instead. That Ph.D. wasn't all it was cracked up to be (and she really sucked at the whole scientist thing), so she dropped out and got a M.S. in forensic toxicology just to get the whole thing over with as soon as possible.

After graduation she got a job with the state of Colorado as their one and only hog farm inspector and spent her days wandering the Eastern Plains shooting the shit with farmers.

After a few years of that, she got bored. And since she was a homeschool mom and actually does love science, she decided to write science textbooks and make online classes for other homeschool moms.

She wrote more than two hundred of those workbooks and was the number one publisher at the online homeschool store many times, but eventually she covered every science topic she could think of and ran out of shit to say.

279

So in 2012 she decided to write fiction instead. That year she released her first three books and started a career that would make her a New York Times bestseller and land her on the USA Today Bestseller's List twenty-one times in the next five years.

In May 2018 MGM Television bought the TV and film rights for five of her books in the Rook & Ronin and Company series' and in March 2019 they offered her and her writing partner, Johnathan McClain, a script deal to write a pilot for a TV show.

Her books have sold millions of copies all over the world, the audio version of her semi-autobiographical book, Eighteen, was nominated for a Voice Arts Award and an Audie Award in 2016 and 2017 respectively, her audiobook, Mr. Perfect, was nominated for a Voice Arts Award in 2017, and her audiobook, Taking Turns, was nominated for an Audie Award in 2018. In 2019 her book, Total Exposure, was nominated for a Romance Writers of America RITA Award.

Johnathan McClain is her first (and only) writing partner and even though they are worlds apart in just about every way imaginable, it works.

She lives on a ranch in Central Colorado with her family.

Printed in May 2019
by Rotomail Italia S.p.A., Vignate (MI) - Italy